About the Author

D.R. Binkley is a retired thirty-year veteran bilingual teacher. He enjoys reading, writing, crossword puzzles and collecting Karakuri boxes. He lives in the San Francisco Bay Area with his wife and son and their cairn terrier, Oliver.

Au Contraire
The Story of an Identity Crisis

D. R. Binkley

Au Contraire
The Story of an Identity Crisis

Vanguard Press

A CIP catalogue record for this title is
available from the British Library.

ISBN 978 1 83794 183 4

This is a work of fiction. Names, characters, businesses, places, events
and incidents are either the product of the author's imagination or
used in a fictitious manner. Any resemblance to actual persons, living
or dead, or actual events is purely coincidental.

*Vanguard Press is an imprint of
Pegasus Elliot Mackenzie Publishers Ltd.*
www.pegasuspublishers.com

First Published in 2024

**Vanguard Press
Sheraton House Castle Park
Cambridge England**

Printed & Bound in Great Britain

For Lisa and Daniel

Many thanks to everyone at Pegasus Publishers who helped publish this book.

I

October, 1994

No. Such a simple word. Only two phonemes. One consonant and one long vowel. A single syllable. And yet so hard to say sometimes. Why is that? Why did Morty find it so hard to say no to people? Was it his inherent desire to please them? To be non-confrontational? To avoid letting people down? He found himself saying yes when he wanted to say no. Then he found himself doing things that he didn't want to do. He finally came to the conclusion that he just had to say no. Sometimes at least. He had to learn to please himself. To not let himself down. That became Morty's resolution, on that day, to just say no. His mantra became the polar opposite of the popular Nike shoe company slogan: Just don't do it.

There's no time like the present to put a newly minted philosophy into practice, Morty thought. And the present was a sunny Sunday in early October of 1994. Sunday. Ever since he could remember his mother had dragged him off to church every Sunday. He would have to attend Sunday school while his mother went to the early service, then when he turned thirteen he had to go to the service along with her. While his father was still in the picture, he was usually off playing golf or watching the Raiders on TV while drinking beer with his buddies. Not this Sunday though. This Sunday Morty was going to put a stop to it. He was going to refuse to go to church. He was going to say no, and he was going to do what he wanted to do on Sunday for once.

Clarissa Phalen opened the door to her son's room and saw that he was still in bed. She bustled in and gave him a shake and said with irritation, "Get up and get dressed, Morty, you're going to make us late again."

"No."

"Are you sick?"

Morty thought about saying yes. He'd faked being sick before, but then the tiresome Sunday ritual would just continue. He wanted to finally make a clean break. "No, I'm fine, I'm just not going to church any more, that's all."

At first she said nothing. Then she turned in a huff and stalked off saying, "I need a cigarette." She came back a few moments later with a lighted Marlboro Light in her hand and stopped in his doorway. Morty turned to look at her. She took a deep drag and blew a long plume of smoke into his room. She knew he hated that. She raised her gravelly voice and spat out shrilly, "I'm trying to raise you to be a good God-fearing Christian and this is the thanks I get. I'm gonna be late; we'll talk about this when I get home," then turned and marched off. He heard the rapid clack clack of her heels on the hardwood floors as she rushed around gathering her things. A few moments later he heard the front door slam. As soon as the door slammed home, Morty leapt out of bed, threw on his jeans and a T-shirt, pulled on thick socks, and laced up his hiking boots. He was out the door shortly after his mother turned the corner at the end of their street.

Ari Grunbergwas a shy, introverted teen. A loner. At fifteen he was six foot three – a good six inches taller than the majority of his peers. With his mop of curly black hair, nerdy black-framed glasses perched on an all too prominent aquiline nose, and a bad case of acne, he stood out like a redwood among oaks and madrones. Having always been rather anti-social, he was often teased mercilessly by the bullies at school. He spent most of his time at school in the library with his head buried in books. Morty loved to read. He was smart and got good grades in the subjects he liked, but only Cs at best in those he found uninteresting. Socially, he was inept. Morty actually got teased about how smart he was. Why is it that it's not cool to be smart?

Morty's home life was no respite for him either. His parents had gotten divorced when he was ten and his deadbeat father had moved to Seattle. Morty had rarely seen him in the intervening years. His mother, who had gone back to using her maiden name Phalen, was a borderline alcoholic. She was functional enough during the day to hold down a job as a nurse, ironically enough, but then when she got home she'd quaff two bottles of cheap wine, red or white it didn't matter, every evening without fail. When she was well into her second bottle she'd be tipsy and inarticulate, slurring her speech and constantly repeating herself. It was exasperating to try to hold a conversation with her. The worst part was that she'd often get verbally abusive with Morty. She'd crash most nights by eight sprawled askew on her bed yet somehow manage to pull herself together enough in the morning to get to work, not remembering much of what had gone on the night before. It was kind of like living with two different people – the daytime mom and the nighttime mom – and conversations often had to be repeated as if they'd never occurred. Schizoid was what Morty deemed it.

Morty's only escape, other than losing himself in one of his novels, was the outdoors and his love of nature. From now on he was going to spend his Sundays in his own sanctum. Instead of sitting in an uncomfortable pew listening to a banal, boring, sanctimonious sermon, he would hike out to Brushy Peak and on to the Vasco Caves. He'd found a rock tucked away in a hidden spot among the Vaqueros Sandstone outcroppings and valley oak trees that was flat on top like a miniature mesa. Whenever he could get away he'd hike out there, sit on this perfect natural bench, his throne, and smoke a joint. Then he'd just meditate and take in the view of the caves around him and out over the Livermore Valley. That was Morty's idea of communing with the divine. That was his idea of a Sunday well spent.

While Morty was relaxing on his natural stone bench enjoying the sunshine and the view out over the sandstone outcroppings that had been eroded over the centuries, his mother was five miles to the west sitting alone on a pew in a postmodern church with a wooden cross standing on an altar in front of a tall, narrow, stained glass window, listening to the reverend give a sermon on how God created the world in seven days' time and what it felt like to become a born again Christian.

Morty pondered the Vasco Caves region. The huge Vaqueros Sandstone outcroppings sprawl across the rolling California golden hills like the twisted broken spine of a gargantuan dinosaur, the scattered vertebrae pocked with osteoporosis to an advanced degree resulting in innumerable whimsically sculpted nooks and crannies. The rock caves and crevices stand in stark contrast to the three generations of wind turbines lined up like giant white idols on the surrounding hills. Idols to the winds.

He pondered how these natural wonders had been formed. The wind almost always blows at the Vasco Caves. It blows up gustily from the southwest, sweeping over the massive sandstone faces. Who knows what vagaries of the wind currents cause them to slowly blow away this face and not that? Whether it be disturbances of the branches of a tree, the contours of the earth, or the Coriolis effect, the capricious wind blows in infinite swirling patterns. Who knows what subtle chemical anomalies and inconsistencies in the composition and shape of the rock cause specific areas to be more or less subject to the ravages of wind and water? Once the hard exterior crust has been penetrated, a pocket is carved in the soft interior of the sandstone. The pocket continues to catch the wind and water as it grows, while neighboring areas, the crust intact, remain comparatively unscathed. Spherical wrecking ball-sized concretions, formed around ancient organic remains, manifest themselves over eons in the rock faces as the softer surrounding sedimentary rock material is slowly worn away. The wrecking ball-sized spheroids grow ever more round until supporting arm grows too weak. The mass succumbs to the eternal pull of gravity, breaks free, and rolls down to the base of the slope like Sisyphus' boulder. Mountains are thrust up and worn down as the Earth follows its endless cycles of formation and deformation.

The bulbous fifty-foot high sandstone outcroppings are continually undercut by wind and water. Feng Shui forming ovoid grottos. To enter one of the caverns is a singular experience. No two caves are alike. One, a mammoth oyster with a crystal ball-sized concretion, like a pearl, lying in the center. Another with walls covered with calcium leaching like white lichen wallpaper, Escheresque ginseng-daikon motif wainscoting, and swallow nest molding. A third with matching stone pillars, precariously thin in the middle, and a medicine ball-sized, red lichen-covered concretion hung on swirl-frescoed walls. A walk through the Vasco Caves was like a tour of nature's sculpture garden, landscaped with valley oaks, buckeyes, black sage, and sticky monkey flower. Watered by underground springs.

Morty delighted in exploring the caves. Around every bend was another gallery of nature's art. After daydreaming for a while, Morty would get the urge to go exploring.

Ever since Morty was a youngster he'd loved to fish and catch frogs, salamanders, turtles, lizards, and snakes. Over the years he'd gotten very good a fashioning his own poles, tying flies, and using nooses and forked sticks to capture these creatures. In his room at home he maintained a large aquarium with a few different species of small native fish. He preferred catching native specimens to buying tropical fish at aquarium stores. When any fish grew too big for his tank, he'd take it back to the place where he'd caught it and let it go. He also kept several terrariums and vivariums with specially designed environments to house his rotating collection of amphibians and reptiles.

Morty fondly and vividly remembered his first encounter with a rattlesnake. It was only a baby about fifteen inches long and it lay stretched out in the middle of the path basking in the sun. Using a forked stick to pin its neck, it had been easy to capture. When he brought it home and showed the baby rattler with its cute little nub of a rattle to his mother, she freaked out. She emphatically and categorically would not allow him to keep it in her house and wanted Morty to kill it. He refused and took it out to a sunny part of the slope behind their home and let it go. After all, rattlesnakes have their place in nature and a role to play too, even if it were only to freak out lame moms.

Since that day Morty considered it a challenge to capture any small rattlesnake he came across. He didn't dare mess with the adult snakes. It was a dangerous game, but he was thrilled by the adrenaline rush he got when taking on one of the venomous serpents. He had successfully caught a few juvenile rattlers during his many sojourns into the hills. He never again brought them home for that would probably have been the last straw with his mother. No, after the challenge and the rush of the battle to capture one, he'd stare into its reptilian eyes while holding it by its neck and then gently toss it away from him into the brush and watch it slither away.

When Morty got home at around four, his mother was waiting for him. As he rushed past her on the way to his room, she said, "We need to talk." Once glance was enough for Morty to tell that she was already three sheets to the wind. She stood leaning against the kitchen doorjamb, with her shoulder length dirty blond hair rather disheveled and that laconic look in her watery blue eyes. Morty said nothing. She followed him down the hall to his room asking, "Did you hear me?"

"Yeah, I heard you." He sat on the end of his bed as she came and propped herself in his doorway, a short glass of some clear alcohol on ice dangling lazily in her right hand. Probably vodka.

"I missed you at church today. I want you to come with me next Sunday."

"No."

"I'm worried about your spiritual development. You need to hear the word of God, Morty. It's only once a week for God's sake. Is that too much to ask?"

"It's boring. There's nothing for me there."

"Reverend Bunyan gives an excellent sermon every Sunday. I wish you had heard him today. Today's sermon was all about how he discovered the true meaning of Christ and came to be a born again Christian. He said becoming a born again Christian is like putting on a new suit of clothes. You feel newly alive and ready to go out into the world and do good."

"I'm comfortable in these old jeans and this well-worn T-shirt, thank you very much."

"I'm serious, Morty. This is about your salvation. You need to embrace Jesus so you can be saved and enter the kingdom of heaven when you pass on. You have to have faith."

"That's just it – I have no faith. I don't believe a word they say. All this rot about Jesus being the only son of God and Christianity being the one true religion is a lot of brainwashing. I don't believe a word of it. I wasn't born yesterday. I've done a lot of reading. I'm not about to swallow that crap."

"You watch your mouth, Morty Schwarzkopf. I won't have you blaspheming the Lord in this house."

"No 'Lord'," Morty used his fingers to make the quotation marks sign in the air when he said the word 'Lord', "gives a damn what I say."

His mother just shook her head slowly and finally said, "You're going to hell in a handbasket, young man, if you don't come back into the fold."

"I don't believe in hell, or heaven either for that matter, so you can't scare me with that. It doesn't make sense anyway to try to use all these scare tactics to frighten people into believing in God. Woo, beware! If you don't believe you won't go to heaven, you'll be doomed to eternal damnation and forever dwell with the devil in the burning flames of hell. What a load of nonsense. I thought your God was merciful and forgiving."

"You're going to church with me next Sunday and every Sunday from now on. You need it more than ever 'cause you're heading down the path of evil."

"No, I'm not! Never! Leave me alone!" Morty leapt up and reached the door in one long stride, and as his mother drew back, he slammed the door in her face.

Morty had done a lot of reading about comparative religions and philosophy. It was his firm belief that all religions were seeking the same thing and that no single one was superior to another. Everyone was seeking solace in a sometimes scary world and all paths to that end were equally valid. Therefore it was also impossible for Morty to 'have faith' and embrace any single path to the exclusion of all others, especially when exclusion meant denial of their validity. He felt it was a supreme act of arrogance, ethnocultural centricity, and really xenophobia to do so. When it came right down to it, Morty felt that he was basically an agnostic. He believed that all of the religions were attempts by humans to explain the world and find truth, but that none of them truly knew the truth and surely no single religion had a corner on it. It wasn't that he had anything against people believing in a religion. If people found solace in their beliefs and it led them to do good, then for them it was true and good. But that didn't make it a universal truth. And just because you had faith and believed in your religion, it didn't mean that you had to deny the validity of all other religions and call people who believed in them heathens. Morty couldn't get behind that.

Every Sunday Morty's mother tried to coax him into going to church with her, but he steadfastly continued to say, "No." Then came the rainy Sunday morning in late December that would change the course of Morty's life.

He'd always enjoyed exploring the caves in the rainy months more than at other times of the year. He was walking around on the muddy, water saturated ground in an area of the caves he'd not explored before when he saw a spire-shaped rock formation about six feet tall that was shaped remarkably like a phallus. As he approached the curiously shaped rock, he came around a stand of densely foliated black sage and spied a deep cave at the base of a huge sandstone dome. Just then the wind picked up and rain started coming down in sheets. Morty scampered over the slippery earth, slipping and nearly falling twice, and took refuge in the cave. The mouth of the cave was about eight feet high and twelve feet wide, forming a ragged oval shape. In the dim light, Morty scanned the dusky interior of the cavity. It was formed like the inside of an eggshell cut in half longitudinally and went back a good six feet. He sat down on the dry powdery dirt floor.

The rain was coming down even harder now, pelting the ground. Morty sat and watched the puddles forming on the mist-shrouded landscape and running together on the water logged earth. It had been an unusually rainy December for the Livermore area that year. Water dripped steadily from the lip of the cave into a depression that had eroded just outside the opening over the years. He watched as the water reached the rim of the shallow depression and flowed over and down a gradual slope to his right. After about twenty minutes the downpour began to slacken until only a light rain continued. Morty decided it was time to move on.

As he hopped over the water filled depression toward a large cube like rock on the other side, a great mass of water soaked soil gave way under his foot and went sliding down the slope, taking him sprawling down with it. Morty was shaken and his backside was soaked and covered in mud, but he was unhurt. As he scrambled to his feet his boot scraped away the soil covering the edge of a shiny object. Reaching down, he dug away the rest of the soil around it and picked it up. It was a gold coin.

He scraped away the surface dirt around where he'd found the gold piece and after twenty minutes of excited searching he had found two more coins. His heart was pounding with the excitement of his discovery. Morty spent the next hour scrambling around in the mudslide but was unable to find any more coins. He was exhausted. He clambered up the gentle slope to the right of the rock and back around to the cave. He was drenched through and through, his boots and his jeans caked with mud, but he hardly even noticed. He was transfixed by the gold pieces.

Using his T-shirt Morty cleaned off the coins as best he could. He couldn't get the dirt out of the many tiny spaces around the reeded edges of the rims. When he finished they were shiny and untarnished and, except for a few scratches and some slight signs of wear here and there, almost like new. All three were of the same type. They had reeded edges on both sides. One side pictured a mounted horseman twirling a lariat. Across the top in a downward arcing curve were the words 'CALIFORNIA GOLD'. Along the bottom and curving upward it said 'TEN DOLLARS'. Underneath the ground upon which the prancing horse stood was the date, 1850. That was apparently the obverse of the coin. On the reverse was an eagle with its wings spread wide, a shield on its breast, three arrows grasped in its left talons, and an olive branch in its right. In a curve along the top edge it said 'BALDWIN & CO' and curving upward along the bottom, 'SAN FRANCISCO'. Ten dollar gold coins struck in 1850.

When Morty got home his mother lit into him screeching, "Where in the hell have you been? Look at you! Haven't I told you over and over to get home in time for dinner? Now your dinner's cold. What the hell's wrong with you, you little shit? I swear I'm gonna kick you outta this house and make you fend for yourself if you don't straighten up and fly right."

It was a one-sided exchange. She was already three-sheets-to-the-wind, and Morty had learned that there was no point in responding when his shrew of a mother got going on one of her drunk tantrums. It would only make matters worse. He went into his room and locked the door. His mother continued to rant and rave for a while telling him he'd better get out there and eat his dinner or else, but Morty was intent on stashing the coins he'd found. He planned to return to the caves with the military surplus spade his father had left behind when he deserted them to dig up the spot thoroughly to see if there might be more coins buried there. It might be some days before he'd have a chance to get back there for he'd be back in school soon. He stuck the coins in an old white sock and tied it off.

He surveyed his room for a spot to hide the them. He thought about hiding them under his mattress. *How original! No one would think of looking there.* But seriously, there wasn't any place better and his mother was unlikely to turn up the mattress. Morty turned the mattress up on its side and leaned it against the wall. He used his jackknife to make a four-inch slit in the bottom of the middle of the mattress and stuffed the sock of coins up in there. That was a stroke of genius, he felt. It would be easy to overlook the slit if someone did look under the mattress. He replaced the mattress on the bed, straightened the sheets and covers, and went out to face the music.

The following Sunday was New Year's Day, and school resumed on Tuesday, January third. Morty's first week back was long and boring after the excitement of his winter break. When Saturday finally rolled around, Morty went to a coin dealer he'd found in the Yellow Pages. He wanted to find out how much the coins were worth and try to sell one of them.

Diablo Coins on First Street in Old Town Livermore was within easy riding distance on his bicycle. As Morty pushed open the door he noticed a sign in the window that said 'We Buy Gold'. That was a promising start. The man behind a desk was busy helping another customer, so Morty busied himself looking at the coins in the glass display cases that lined the walls on both sides and the left portion of the rear wall with enough space behind them for the owner or employees to walk behind them and get access to the coins on display. There was a desk with a bright lamp and mounted magnifying glass that could be lowered and raised on it in the right rear corner. A walkway down the middle led to a couple of dark rooms at the rear of the shop.

While Morty pretended to be interested in the old silver dollars displayed in the case along the right hand wall, he occasionally stole glances at the proprietor who was seated at the desk examining some coins while the customer sat in a chair in front of the desk with his back to Morty. The owner was a plump, middle-aged fellow, balding with a large shiny dome of a head and just a few wisps of brown hair down the sides and combed across his pate. Once, he glanced up just as Morty was peeking at him and before Morty turned his head back to the display, he caught a fleeting glimpse of a pair of none too friendly, closely set, beady little brown eyes that looked incongruous in his bulbous head. That and a receding double chin under a pair of thinly compressed lips left an unfavorable impression on Morty.

"May I help you?"

Pretending to be engrossed in the coin display, Morty had not realized that the other customer had concluded his business. He'd brought only one of the coins he'd found initially to test the market. He took it out of his pocket. Holding out the coin he said, "Yes, I'd like to ascertain the value of this gold coin." He'd rehearsed this line and thought the use of the word 'ascertain' would impress the coin dealer with his vocabulary. The coin dealer held out his hand and Morty deposited the coin in it. Turning it over in his stubby fingers he remarked, "This is a very interesting coin. Where did you get it?"

"My grandfather left it to me in his will," Morty lied.

"Are you interested in selling it?"

"That all depends on how much you're willing to pay."

"Well, let's see. This coin was minted by a private company – Baldwin and Company – in eighteen-fifty in San Francisco, as you can plainly see. The San Francisco branch of the United States Mint did not begin minting coins until eighteen-fifty-four Of course, coins produced by a U.S. mint are much more valuable. This coin is likely approximately the equivalent of the eagles produced by the U.S. mints. But let us first, er… ascertain if it is genuine."

He took a small bottle of some acid chemical out of the left hand drawer of his desk. The top was like an eyedropper and squeezing the bulb with the tip in the fluid, he drew up a small amount. Laying the coin on his desk under the light, he dropped a single drop on the coin and observed it, apparently looking for a reaction of some kind, but nothing happened. There was no reaction at all. Was that good or bad? Morty wondered.

"It's genuine, all right. I would say it's an alloy of most likely approximately ninety percent gold and ten percent copper. Without melting it down it's impossible to tell the exact proportions of the alloy." Looking up and scrutinizing Morty, he suddenly said, "Fritz Utrecht," and extended his hand.

"Morty Schwartzkopf, pleased to meet you Mr. Utrecht."

"Call me Fritz."

"Okay… so… it's not pure gold?"

"No, such an alloy is typical of coins of that era. Today, with advances in technology, it's possible to mint gold coins that are ninety-nine point nine nine percent pure gold, but back in those days it was necessary to alloy it with some other metal, usually copper, in order to increase the hardness of the gold, which is a particularly dense, soft, and malleable metal."

He put the coin on a scale.

"It weighs almost exactly half an ounce, which means there is most likely ten percent less than half an ounce of gold in it. I don't have any information of the specific composition of this type of coin. The current price of gold is three hundred eighty-six dollars an ounce, or so it was when I checked it this morning." Taking up a calculator and punching a few keys he continued, "So the gold value of this coin is about a hundred and seventy-four dollars." The coin dealer scrutinized Morty's face to note his reaction to that pronouncement. Being ignorant of the value of coins, Morty was calculating how much money the coins he'd found would bring.

"Hmm," was his only response.

Reaching for a red volume on a shelf alongside his desk the dealer went on, "Of course we also have to consider the numismatic value."

"Pardon me, the numis – what?" queried Morty.

"Numismatic… the value of the coin to collectors."

"Oh."

Leafing through the coin guidebook, he stopped at a page, then laid the book face down and picked up the coin again. He pulled down the magnifier, tilted the light, and carefully examined the condition again. After a while he remarked, "This coin has a few scratches and some slight wear on the raised areas, most likely bag marks from having been stored and transported in a bag with other coins. It may have been in circulation for a brief period of time – not long for it is in quite good condition. I would grade it as AU."

Morty said, "I'm sorry, I'm not familiar with that term."

"Oh, right. AU stands for 'Almost Uncirculated'. That is to say this coin was not in day to day circulation for long if at all."

"I see."

Consulting the coin book again, he ran his index finger down the page stopping about halfway down. He tilted his head back, closing his eyes and pursing his lips, appearing to calculate mentally. Then he put the book face down on the desk again. "I would put the value of this coin at one thousand six hundred dollars." Once again he watched for Morty's reaction.

"Really!" Morty gasped in disbelief. He was seeing dollar signs.

"So, would you be wanting to sell this coin? Because I can write you a check for sixteen hundred dollars right now if you should be so inclined."

"Yes, I would," Morty said, unable to suppress a smile. "But I'd prefer cash."

"I'm sorry, but I don't keep that kind of cash on hand. I can assure you that my check is good. It's drawn from a local bank – the Bank of the West over on Second. You can go over there and cash it – of course today is Saturday and they are closed so if you'd prefer to wait until Monday…"

"No, I guess a check would be all right."

"All right," Fritz said, drawing his checkbook over and picking up a pen.

As he filled out the check, Morty sat beside himself in disbelief at his good fortune. He was going to have a good deal of money to spend for the first time in his life.

"Now I'll just need to see a picture ID and have you fill out his form with your name and address."

Morty was a little taken aback. "Why do you need my name and address?"

"It's just a formality… in case someone were to report a coin such as this one to have been stolen."

"I didn't steal it!"

"Of course you didn't. You inherited it. It's just standard procedure for all transactions of this kind, I can assure you," Fritz cooed in his most ingratiating manner. Morty took out his wallet, removed his school ID, and handed it to Fritz. While he filled out the form the coin dealer noted Morty's full name and the school he attended. When Morty was done, Fritz handed back his ID along with the check and put the gold coin on the corner of his desk. He put his hands on the arms of his chair and raised his ponderous bulk with difficulty. He extended his hand and said, "It's a pleasure doing business with you, Morty," as Morty shook it.

"Likewise," Morty answered, releasing Fritz's hand and turning to go.

As Morty grasped the door handle and pulled the door open, Fritz said mischievously, "Oh Morty," and when Morty turned back, "you wouldn't happen to have inherited any more of those coins, would you?" Once again he observed Morty's expression keenly.

Flustered, Morty shook his head a little too vigorously and squeaked out a flaccid, "No," and hurriedly exited the shop.

When Fritz Utrecht's partner, Jim Burt, came in bearing lunch, Fritz was beaming. "You won't believe the transaction I just made. This kid came in to sell this coin," he said handing the coin to Jim. "Have you ever seen one of those before?"

"No... never."

"They were minted in the city during the gold rush by a private firm, Baldwin and Company, shortly after California became a state. There was a dire need for gold coins as a medium of exchange. The San Francisco Mint didn't begin operations until 1854. Do you have any idea how rare these are? I paid the kid sixteen hundred for it. It's worth upwards of a hundred thousand dollars, maybe more. Steak dinners tonight, Jimmy Boy!"

"Yeah, baby!"

"What's more, I think the kid might have more of them. He says he inherited it from his grandfather, but I don't buy it. When I asked him if he had any more, he was clearly lying when he said no."

"If he does have more to sell, we need to make sure he brings them to us. Did he seem satisfied with the deal?"

"Totally. He was clueless as to its true worth. I sent him out of here with a check for sixteen hundred and he was as happy as a breastfeeding baby."

"Did you get the usual info on him?"

"Naturally. Wait a few weeks and if he doesn't show up again, which I doubt he will with that kind of cash, then pay him a visit. If the address is bogus, you'll have to track him through his school. He goes to Livermore High, and his name is Morty Schwartzkopf. The info's right here."

"Will do."

Morty spent an uneasy weekend anxiously awaiting his chance to get to. the bank to cash the check. Unfortunately, he had some other business to take care of after school on Monday, so he wasn't able to get over to Second Street until after school on Tuesday. The anticipation was killing him. Sixteen hundred dollars, and the prospect of more, maybe much more. He had to get back up there to search for more gold. This was going to allow him a measure of independence he'd never enjoyed. Still, he absolutely had to keep the whole affair secret from his mother. If she got a whiff of the money or his find, she'd demand he give it to her for sure. He would have to avoid any drastic change in his habits and lifestyle or she would surely sniff it out.

When Morty queued up at the bank on Tuesday afternoon he wondered what recourse he'd have if the check were no good. When he got to the teller, a pretty petite blonde, he handed her the check and said, "I'd like to cash this please."

"Do you have an account with us?"

"No."

"Okay. Sixteen hundred dollars is a lot of money to be carrying around with you. Perhaps you'd like to open one?"

Morty considered that for a moment, then said, "Yes, please."

"Great, I'll call our manager over and she can help you."

Morty hesitated. What risk was there in opening a bank account? It sounded like a good idea actually. His money would be safe and he wouldn't have to hide it and worry about it. He knew his mother banked at Bank of America so there was little risk of her somehow finding out about his account at Bank of the West. "All right, yeah."

"If you'll just take a seat at that desk over there," she said pointing to a desk across the way, "she'll be with you in a moment."

Morty turned and walked over to the desk and sat down. In a few minutes a portly woman approached and sat down at the desk opposite him.

"I understand you want to open an account with us."

"Yes."

"May I ask how old you are?"

Morty wasn't prepared for this. Not really accustomed to lying, he told the truth. "I'm fifteen."

"We would need a parent or guardian's consent as cosignatory in order for you to open an account as a minor."

"Oh, I see. Can I just cash this check without opening an account?"

"I'm afraid we won't be able to do that either. I'm sorry."

"That's all right," Morty muttered as he got up to leave. But it wasn't all right. Why did something always have to crop up to block his way? Just when he thought things were looking up big time. Well, there was no help for it. He'd just have to go back to the coin shop and demand payment in cash.

By the time he rode over to Diablo Coins, it was after five and it was closed. Morty rode home dejectedly, feeling sorry for himself, thinking in the back of his mind that all along he knew it was too good to be true.

On Wednesday, Morty rode over to Diablo Coins after school. At first he thought Mr. Utrecht had a customer, but then he realized that the other fellow also worked there. He was a stoutly built guy with a blond crew cut, blue eyes, and a square jaw. Fritz Utrecht introduced him to Morty as his partner, Jim Burt. They shook hands. "Now, how can we help you, Morty?"

Drawing the check out of his wallet, Morty related what had happened at the bank, "They wouldn't cash the check for me since I'm still a minor. Can you pay me in cash instead?"

"Oh, I hadn't thought of that," Fritz replied. "You look rather older than your age. Of course, that's no problem. We'll have to make a trip to the bank." Glancing at his gold Rolex watch he said, "It's four ten now and the bank's just a few blocks away. Jim, would you mind running over there to get Morty his money? Sixteen hundred dollars."

"No problem." Without delay he headed for the door.

Morty had spent a rather uncomfortable half hour in desultory conversation with Fritz Utrecht when Jim Burt finally returned. He'd kept wishing a customer would enter the shop to relieve the tension, but not a single one did.

Burt took a thick envelope out of his jacket pocket and handed it to Morty. "Here you go, sonny, sixteen hundred bucks. You're a rich man."

"Thank you. If you don't mind, I'll just be on my way. I need to be getting home."

"Don't you want to count it?" Jim asked.

"Gee, I suppose I should, no offense."

"None taken."

Stepping up to a display case Morty counted out the sixteen hundred dollar bills. Seeing such a pile of hundreds was mind-boggling to him. It was way more money than he'd ever had in his life, that's for sure.

When he finished, Fritz smiled and said, "So you see we are as good as our word. Now put that envelope in a safe place and be careful on your way home. If you should have any more coins to sell in the future, we'd be glad to do business with you again. Take care now."

As Morty headed out the door he said, "Thanks again," and closed the door behind him. It was all he could do to keep from letting out a whoop. As he rode home all glowing and warm with his success, he pondered what he should do with the money and how to conceal it from his mother. He'd gotten pretty clever at hiding things in his room once he realized that his mother occasionally searched it. He thought the best thing would be to tape the envelope full of money under his dresser. That was how he'd concealed his stash of weed until he realized that the Purple Kush strain he habitually purchased was so fragrant that even if he double bagged it he could still smell it, especially when he was near his dresser. After that he'd hidden it in their garage, which was draftier. He wouldn't have that problem with the money.

A couple of weeks passed uneventfully. Morty was careful not to alter his usual routine. He'd used duct tape to tape the envelope full of money underneath his dresser, taking three hundred dollars with him whenever he left the house in case he should want some money to spend. Just such an occasion occurred on the evening of Friday, January 27th.

His mother had sent him out with some money to buy a take-home dinner. As he was waiting for their food in the front of the restaurant, Morty saw Christy Matthews seated at a table with her mother, her father, and her brother. Christy was a girl Morty had had a crush on since freshman year, unbeknownst to her. He'd never had the gumption to talk to her and he figured she probably didn't even know he existed. On a whim, he conceived of the idea of paying their bill without their knowledge. He told the hostess what he wanted to do and she spoke to their waitress. The waitress brought the check over and Morty paid the cashier. He had a great sense of satisfaction at having the money to do it. He wished he'd be able to see the look on their faces when at the end of their dinner, the waitress informed them that their bill had been paid by an unknown benefactor. He was delighted with the idea that he could use his riches in such a way. When his food was ready, he paid and left. He was starting to feel quite good about himself for a change.

The following Thursday, Morty was finishing his homework at the kitchen table when he heard his mother pull into the garage. A moment later she came into the kitchen. She put a bag of groceries she was carrying on the counter, turned to him and said, "I ran into Cindy Matthews at the supermarket a little while ago, and she told me something interesting. Do you know what it was, Morty? She told me that you paid for her family's dinner at Chi Chi's the other night. And I said, 'Really? I wonder what got into Morty and where did he get the money to do something like that?' and she said, 'And why do you suppose he did it?' Well, Morty, what do you have to say for yourself?"

Morty was speechless, his face turning red, his head growing hot. He'd been caught completely off guard. How had they known it was he who had paid their bill? Since when was his mother acquainted with Mrs. Matthews? He couldn't think of any response. Finally he stammered, "I just thought it would be a nice gesture, Christy and I being schoolmates and all."

"But the money, Morty. Where did you get the money? I didn't give you enough to pay for their dinner as well. In fact, you brought me back my change. Well?"

"I had a little money saved up, you know birthday money and such."

"Let me see your wallet."

"No!" She made a move to grab his wallet from his pants' pocket and he grabbed her wrists. Struggling with her he shouted, "Stop, you have no right, it's mine!"

"Morty Schwarzkopf, you give me that wallet right this instant!" The look on her face was hard for Morty to bear. There was nothing for it. He let go of her wrists, took his wallet out and slapped it on the table saying petulantly, "Fine! Take it then, you bitch!"

She slapped him across the face screaming, "Shut your trap!" Morty shot up, violently sending the chair tumbling as he shoved it back. He raised his right arm and clenched his fist as if he was about to pop his mother one.

"Go ahead," she taunted. "I'll have you up on assault charges so fast it will make your stomach churn."

"And what about you!" Morty screamed at the top of his lungs. He was quivering with rage. Slowly, he lowered his arm. His mother snatched up the wallet and looked inside. Her eyes grew wide when she saw two hundreds and two twenties in it. "Where did you get this money? You tell me right now."

"It's a long story and I don't feel like telling it."

"You're gonna tell me where you got this money, sooner or later, Morty Schwartzkopf. For right now, I'm taking it."

"You have no right, it's mine. I hate you!"

After a tension filled pause, she said, surprisingly calmly, "Oh you hate me, do you? We'll see about that. How about if you go live with your father?" She took a bottle of wine out of the bag, uncorked it, and poured herself a glass. "Yes, I think that's a great idea. I'll give him a call in the morning. It's about time he put in some time raising you." Morty stormed off to his room without saying another word. He slammed his door and locked it.

The next day was Friday and Morty didn't see his mother in the morning as he prepared for school. It was strange for her not to be getting ready for work. Morty checked the calendar she kept on the kitchen wall and saw that she had the day off. He made preparations to visit the Vasco Caves after school, going back to his room to change into his boots and load his backpack with the stuff he'd need, including an extra bottle for water and some trail mix for a snack. Fortunately Fridays were early dismissal days at school so that would just give him enough time to get out to the caves for a little while and get back only a bit later than he usually did on those school days when he didn't go straight home.

Clarissa Phalen slept in that morning and had a bit of a headache when she finally dragged herself out of bed around eleven. She fixed herself a Bloody Mary and set about searching Morty's room. She'd made cursory searches of his room before to see if he had any drugs or porn or condoms or anything she should know about, but this time she was determined to make a thorough search. After going through his dresser drawers, his desk drawers, and his closet without finding anything, she sat down on his desk chair and asked herself where she would hide something in the room. His aquarium and terrariums were on stands with open architecture so it wasn't possible to conceal anything there. Surely he hadn't hidden anything under the mattress. She had to check it. She turned the mattress up and balanced it on its side. No, nothing. Looking around some more she noticed the space under the dresser. She got down on her hands and knees and looked under it. It was dark. She groped under there and the back of her hand brushed against something slightly bulky up underneath. She grabbed it and pulled it loose. Sitting back she opened the envelope. It was full of hundred dollar bills.

She sat on the floor in shock trying to wrap her mind around her son's secret stash of money. How in the world? Just then the mattress tumbled over emitting a faint clink. What was that sound? She went over and shook the mattress. There it was again – a slight clinking sound. She patted the mattress to find the source. She found the slit in the underside, reached in and felt the sock. She pulled it out and untied the knot, pouring two gold coins out onto the bedsprings. She saw that they were old coins. The money was shocking enough – she'd thought maybe Morty was selling drugs or something, but what about the gold coins? After her initial disbelief, she thought, *Now it's my turn to hide the money and the coins*. But no. She decided she'd hide the gold coins, but she'd simply deposit the money in her bank account. She counted it. Thirteen hundred dollars. She thought, *Wow, what has that boy been up to? He's in for a real knock down drag out fight when he gets home*. Just then she heard someone at the door.

After school Morty had to get away for a while. He needed some time to himself to collect his thoughts. It'd had been too long since he'd visited his hidden spot at the Vasco Caves. He wanted to dig around some more to see if he could unearth any more coins. He rode his bike out Vasco Road to a spot from which the caves were more easily accessible. He hid it in some brush near a culvert and set out on foot. If he hurried he could spend maybe an hour at the caves and still get home at a reasonable hour. An hour for contemplation, rejuvenation, and perhaps discovery.

When Morty arrived home at just after six and opened the front door, a chaotic scene met his eyes. The living room was a shambles. The furniture was overturned, the sofa was all cut up and the stuffing was strewn about, the framed artwork had been taken down and set on the floor. He went to the phone to call 911. The kitchen had been rifled as well. After giving the police their address, he hung up and went down the hall to his room. His mother was lying on her side in his room. A pool of blood had spread out on the carpet underneath her head. She was dead. Morty went out on the front stoop and sat down to await the police. He buried his head in his hands. His mother was dead, but he could not seem to shed any tears.

The medical examiner's report stated that Clarissa Phalen had died of blunt force trauma to the back of the head. It appeared that she had fallen or been pushed and hit her head on the corner of a large glass terrarium in the room. Hair and blood samples had been taken from the corner of the terrarium and shown to be those of the victim. After the police had finished their investigation of the scene, they took Morty in for questioning. His father had been called in Seattle and was on his way to Livermore.

A homicide inspector by the name of Ian Seare was in charge of the investigation. Morty told him and the other officers present how he'd come home to discover their house in disarray, how he had called the police and then found his mother dead in his room. The police were struck by his seeming emotional detachment from the death of his mother. He told them that they didn't get along well and often fought. Maybe that was a mistake. They asked him to account for his whereabouts during the day. He told them he'd gone to school and then went hiking in the hills for a couple of hours after school. They asked if anyone had gone hiking with him. He told them no, he always went hiking alone. It was clear that Morty was a prime suspect. He began to grow indignant at the tone of the questions and it showed on his face.

They asked him if anything was missing from their home. He hesitated to tell them about the coins he'd found and the money he'd made from selling the one. He wanted to keep that out of their investigation until it occurred to him that he could mislead them. He could tell them he'd found the coins in some other location. It might get them off his back. So he told them he'd found three old gold coins on Brushy Peak one day in December. He told them about how he'd sold one of them to a coin dealer named Fritz Utrecht at his shop called Diablo Coins downtown on First Street. He also told them about his problems cashing their check at the Bank of the West on Second Street and how Fritz Utrecht's partner named Jim Burt had helped him get the money. He told them how he'd hidden the money and coins in his room, but that they were now missing. That seemed to satisfy them at least for the moment. Morty realized that he had given them an avenue to investigate and he breathed a sigh of relief.

Morty was kept at the police station until his father arrived. An officer had searched his backpack while he was being questioned, but nothing incriminating had been found. He was still a prime suspect, but they didn't have enough evidence to hold him. Morty went to stay with his father at a motel. It was the middle of the night and they were both too tired to talk about what had happened, so they decided to get some sleep and save it till the next day.

On Saturday afternoon, Isaac Grunberg and his son went to lunch at a coffee house. Despite the shocking events of the day before, they had both slept soundly for they were both exhausted – Morty from the emotional events of the previous day and the long questioning at the police station, and Isaac from the late night travel. Morty told his father about what had happened since that fateful day in December. Then the conversation moved on to the happenings in their lives for the past three years since they'd last seen each other.

Later in the afternoon they went back to the police station and were allowed to go to the scene of the crime in the company of Inspector Seare so that Morty could collect some of his clothes. The rest of his personal items would have to wait until the investigation had been completed.

Every room in the house and even the garage and Clarrisa's car was in a state of chaos as if a whirlwind had traveled from room to room exposing every possible hiding place. One thing that struck Ian Seare, as he stood in the doorway of Morty's room watching him pack his clothes, was the incongruity of the complete lack of disturbance of the large aquarium and the four terrariums along one wall of the kid's room. Before leaving, Morty fed his fish some flake food, and put some crickets into the terrariums. He also put a small mouse they'd bought at a pet store into the terrarium in which he kept his striped racer snake. The animals would be okay without any more food for quite a few days now that they'd been fed.

On Monday, February 6th, Morty and his father went to Livermore High and withdrew him from school. He was going to live with his father as soon as he was allowed to leave California and collect the rest of his things. Clarissa Phalen's parents had flown in from Arizona to make funeral arrangements, have a crew clean up the house once the investigation was completed, salvage and sell what they could, and contact a realtor about selling the house. They had an uncomfortable meeting over lunch with Morty and Isaac, but fortunately for Morty, they didn't ask him to tell them about his grisly discovery yet again. They had probably gotten the details from some other source if indeed they could bear to hear them at all. They had never been particularly fond of Isaac Grunberg and their suspicions as to his unsuitability as a match for their daughter had been confirmed when they had gotten divorced after eleven rocky years of marriage. They knew that Morty was somewhat of a troubled youth and that he and Clarissa hadn't gotten along well either, nevertheless they still had a soft spot in their hearts for their grandson.

After lunch they pulled Morty aside to speak to him privately and told him that he would always be welcome to come live with them in Phoenix. Morty thanked them and promised to keep it in mind but said he wanted live with his father in Seattle, at least for the time being. They told him that the memorial service would be held at two p.m. at Callaghan Mortuary on Friday, February 10th with the procession and burial to follow at three-thirty at Roselawn Cemetery. They gave him a card with the information on it and said goodbye till then.

Inspector Ian Seare was a tall, strongly-built man in his mid forties with a full head of light brown hair cut short and handsome, regular features. The keen, piercing look in his steel blue eyes was unsettling to suspects under questioning who had something to hide. He had been on the Livermore police force for nineteen years and had been a homicide inspector for the last eleven of those years.

In investigating the scene of the crime, Seare had immediately noted the complete disarrangement of the furnishings of the house. It certainly looked like someone had made a very thorough search of the premises. An examination of the doors and windows revealed no sign of forced entry, however, when questioned about the degree of security maintained at the house, Morty Schwarzkopf had told him that they often left the doors unlocked when they were at home. A foolish practice if that were true, reflected Seare, considering that there had been several break-ins in the area in recent months. Didn't these people read the local newspapers?

The lab test results for fingerprints at the scene had revealed only those of the tenants, Clarissa Phalen and Mortimer Schwartzkopf. In canvassing the neighborhood, the police had talked to all the neighbors on the block. None of them had seen anything out of the ordinary on that day. The medical examiner had fixed the time of death at around noon on Friday, February the 3rd. All of the neighbors in the immediate vicinity of the Phalen residence had been at work at the time, except one. That was a man named Myers who lived across the street and down a few houses and worked the night shift at a factory in Tracy. He was asleep at the time. He hadn't heard anything unusual. A thorough search of the entire house, the grounds, and the field behind the house in hopes of finding additional evidence was made, but it proved to be fruitless. They had Morty go through the house to determine was else might be missing, but other than the fact that the contents of his mother's purse had been dumped on the floor of her bedroom and whatever money had been in her wallet was gone, he said could find nothing missing. Naturally, the police had already made a note of the state of Clarissa Phalen's purse.

At Livermore High the attendance records showed that Morty Schwarzkopf had come to school on Friday, February 3rd. All of the teachers who taught classes in which Morty was enrolled confirmed that he had attended their classes that day. When Seare asked if the students ever left the campus during school hours, he was told that they had an hour for lunch and were allowed to go off campus during that time. None of the staff could say for sure whether or not Morty Schwarzkopf had eaten lunch on campus that day, but they believed he usually did. They couldn't name any friends Schwarzkopf usually hung out with either. Apparently the kid was a loner. He almost always rode his bicycle to school and Seare calculated that it would take ten to fifteen minutes to cover the distance from the high school to the Phalen home, which was situated on the edge of the northern side of Livermore.

When Inspector Seare went to Diablo Coins on Tuesday, only Fritz Utrecht was in. Jim Burt was the legman for the outfit, spending much of his time attending coin shows, evaluating the suitability of coin collections for purchase, and the like. He showed Fritz Utrecht his badge and said, "I'm Inspector Seare of the Livermore

Police and I'm investigating the murder of Clarissa Phalen."

"I read about that in the paper. How may I help you?"

"Ms. Phalen was the mother of a young man by the name of Morty Schwartzkopf. Mr. Schwartzkopf has told us that he sold a gold coin to you on the morning of Saturday, January 7th."

"Yes, sir, indeed he did. I remember it very clearly."

"Would you mind giving me the details of the transaction?"

"Not at all. The young man brought in a rare gold coin that he wanted to sell. He told me he had inherited it from his grandfather. After examining the coin to determine whether or not it was authentic, which it was, I offered to pay him sixteen hundred dollars for it."

"Some valuable coin. You even remember the exact amount you paid for it."

"To be sure, we don't make purchases like that very often nor buy such, how shall I say, unique coins. I've been in this business for twenty-nine years and I had never seen another coin of that type before, then this young fellow shows up with one."

"What makes them so unique?"

"Those coins were struck by a private mint in the early years of the California Gold Rush. There was a dearth of coins as a medium of exchange in the boom city of San Francisco at the time. Through a loophole in federal law, the private minting of these coins was not technically illegal. At the time, the Constitution only prohibited the states from minting coins. That was amended in eighteen sixty-four. These coins helped fill the void for a time, but the public grew suspicious as to the actual amount of gold they contained. That led to their withdrawal from circulation. The great majority of them were melted down when the San Francisco branch of the United States Mint began striking coins in eighteen fifty-four."

"May I see the coin?"

"I'm afraid I can't help you there. My partner has taken it to a coin show in Los Angeles." Reaching for a red coin guidebook he said, "But I can show you a photo of one." He turned to the section on private and territorial gold and leafed through it until he came to the page. Then he turned the book around and held it out to Seare, pointing to the photo and saying, "Here it is; it's this one right here."

Seare looked at the coin and remarked, "Hmm, eighteen-fifty. So these coins are quite rare?"

"Extremely so."

"Would it be possible for you to make a copy of this for me?"

"Certainly, I have a copier in the back room, just a moment." He waddled to the back of the shop, turned on the light of the room on the right and went in. In a few moments he returned with a copy of the page. "Here you go, Detective. Will there be anything else?"

"Just a few more questions. You say he told you he'd inherited the coin?"

"From his grandfather, yes."

"And did you believe him at the time?"

"Hardly. It was pretty obvious it was a cock and bull story."

"He told us he found three gold coins up on Brushy Peak. How likely is that, would you say?"

"I suppose it's possible. There's an old legend about Joaquin Murrieta and his gang having used that area as a hideout when they were passing the place while driving their stolen horses to Mexico, but I never gave it much credence. There are a lot of old legends about Murrieta, his supposed crimes, and places he and his gang used as hideouts."

"Would there be anyone in the area with that type of coin in their collection?"

"Not that I'm aware of, and I highly doubt it. Three coins like that, if indeed there were three, or even just the one. I really don't think so."

"And no one has brought any more of those coins in since?"

"Certainly not."

"Where were you between the hours of ten a.m. and two p.m. on Friday, February third?"

Fritz Utrecht exclaimed incredulously, "Surely you don't think that I had anything to do with this woman's death."

Inspector Seare calmly calmly, "It's just standard procedure in any murder investigation that we ask anyone even remotely connected to the victim to account for his or her whereabouts at the time of the crime, you understand."

"Well, on Friday the third, I was here in my shop, just like I am every Monday through Saturday."

"Is there anyone who can corroborate that?"

"I'm sure if I go over my records and receipts of the day, I can produce a number of customers who were here in the shop during that time period. We have a number of regular customers who know me, and I keep records of all transactions. I believe my partner, Jim Burt, was also in town on that day, let me just check." He glanced at his calendar. "Yes, he was here on the third. He can verify that I was in the shop that day."

"However, he is out of town at the moment, as you previously stated," Seare commented. He went on, "Here is my card. Would you please have him call me when he gets back in town? And if you'd just put together a list of people who can verify that you were in your shop that day, I'd appreciate it. I'll ask Mr. Burt to come in, and he can bring it when he does, all right?"

"Certainly, Inspector, he will be back in town early next week, on Tuesday I think."

"And if anyone else should bring that type of coin in, you'll be sure let me know immediately?"

"Yes, I will, Inspector."

"Thank you and good day."

"You as well, Inspector Seare."

When he got back to the station, Seare assigned three of his men to call all of the coin dealers in the Tri-Valley area with a description of the coin to determine if any of them had had any customers selling that type of coin recently.

Late Wednesday morning, Inspector Seare called Isaac Grunberg at his hotel and asked him to bring his son to the station. When they arrived in his office, he said to Morty, "I want you to take me to the place where you found the coins."

Morty answered, "All right. When?"

"How about right now?"

"Are you sure? It's almost midday; it'll be darn hot out there right now even at this time of the year."

"We'll manage."

"Okay, but we're going to need some water."

Isaac Grunberg intended to tag along as well, but he didn't look like he was in very good shape. At six foot three he was only an inch or so shorter than his son, but he packed a lot more weight and had a considerable paunch. Morty had gotten the looks and curly black hair of his father, but not his eyes, at least as far as eyesight was concerned. At forty-three Isaac still only wore glasses for reading, whereas Morty had had to wear them constantly since he was in eighth grade.

As they made their way out to an unmarked police car, Morty was thinking fast about where he should take them. He had to take them to some place on Brushy Peak that was a plausible location for the gold coins to have been hidden. He knew they could most easily access Brushy Peak from the end of Laughlin Road, so he directed the detective to drive there. They parked near a dilapidated farmhouse and Morty led them to a trail. It was hot and it was a long, winding climb up close to the summit with a gain of about a thousand feet of elevation. Sure enough, Isaac fell behind huffing and puffing. The detective was quite fit and seemed to be able to deal with the heat well too. Morty was wearing running shoes, but his father was wearing street shoes. Seare's shoes looked reasonably comfortable, but he was sure his father was going to have sore feet when this was over.

Morty had spent a lot of time trekking around the slopes of Brushy Peak when he'd first started exploring the area, but in recent years he'd always gone out to the Vasco Caves. At an elevation of approximately seventeen hundred feet, Brushy Peak surpasses the surrounding hills in height. It got its name because its slopes are sporadically covered with coast live oak trees and sagebrush in contrast to the neighboring rolling hills that are covered only with verdant grasses in the winter and spring, such as the native needlegrass and creeping wildrye, as well as many non-native species like wild oats and soft chess. Brushy Peak is also studded with numerous sandstone rock outcrops that serve as homes for predatory raptors and once served as hiding places for bandits in the old west.

As they hiked, Morty tried to think of a good place to take them. It would have to be a crevice in a rock since there would be no evidence of digging in the ground. He remembered a cool rock formation he'd once come across. Now if he could only find it again. As they neared the peak on the south side, Morty led them around to the eastern side. His father was still clambering up the south slope. They were all quite hot and sweaty. Finally Morty spied the rock formation he remembered. It was a dome-shaped rock that had split in two, creating a deep, dark four-inch wide crevice between the two halves of the dome. Morty stopped and pointed at the crevice, telling Seare, "The gold was in a bag, which was shoved way back in this crevice." Then he took a step back, wiped the perspiration off his brow with the sleeve of his T-shirt, and stood facing the inspector with his arms across his chest.

"You found them in there?"

"Yeah."

"It's dark in there. How could you see something was in there?"

"I always carry a little penlight in my backpack when I go hiking."

Isaac came up to them breathing heavily, and stopping, he leaned over with his hands on his knees.

Inspector Seare went on, "Why did you think to shine your light in there? I mean why would you think to do that?"

"I don't know, curiosity I guess."

"Curiosity. So you shone your light in there, and what did you see?"

"It looked like a small, off white-colored bag."

"So what did you do then?"

"I reached into the crack and pulled it out. Then, I opened the bag and found the gold pieces inside."

Seare's steel blue eyes bored into Morty's and Morty looked away. He could feel his pulse racing.

Seare said, "I see. And the bag, what did you do with it?"

"It was falling apart, disintegrating actually, so I threw it away."

"You threw it away? Where? Out here?"

Morty hesitated. "No, I threw it in the trash when I got home."

"Unhuh. So you were able to lift a bag, which was disintegrating mind you, and which had heavy gold coins in it, out of this crevice, without it falling apart? Is that what you're telling me?"

"Well... ach, I feel lightheaded..." Morty put his left hand on his forehead. "I need to rest for a moment." He put his right hand on the rock to steady himself and then bent his elbow, turning as he did so, and leaned back against the rock. He felt faint, and his face was flushed. He breathed deeply for a couple of minutes with his eyes closed and his head back.

The inspector said, "That's all right, take your time." It was plain to Seare that Morty was lying. His physical symptoms and body language were a dead giveaway. And if Ari Grunbergwas lying about where he'd found the gold pieces, what else might he be lying about?

After a few more minutes, Morty shook his head and said, "I'm sorry, where were we?"

Seare looked around at the scenic view for a while then said, "Never mind, if you feel all right now, let's head back."

Isaac exclaimed, "Already? You mean we came all the way out here just so you could ask a few questions? Couldn't we have done that in your office?"

"I wanted to see the place for myself and hear what your son had to say for himself on the spot, so I could draw my own conclusions."

"And what have you concluded?" Isaac asked.

Seare replied cryptically, "I am not disposed to share that with you at the present time. It'll be in my report," and headed back the way they'd come. Isaac only shook his head and muttered, "At least I'm getting some much needed exercise," then turning to Morty said, "Come on, Morty."

Morty was surprised at how many people attended his mother's memorial service and her burial. He hadn't realized that his mother had had so many friends and acquaintances. The police had spoken to a number of them shortly after Clarissa's death asking if they knew of anyone who bore her a grudge or of any confrontations she'd had.

When the time came, Morty gently laid a bouquet of five white roses on her coffin after it had been partially lowered into the grave. They were his mother's favorite flowers. The fact that Morty didn't shed tears at any point during the entire proceeding was conspicuous. After the service, he had to stand there with his father while all the people filed by to express their condolences, which made him very uncomfortable. He was glad when it was over and they could leave.

On Monday, February 13th, Isaac got a call at their motel from Inspector Seare asking him and Morty to come to the police station again. When they got there, Detective Seare said, "I have your address and phone number in Seattle, Mr. Schwartzkopf, in case I need to contact you or your son concerning this case. We have completed our investigation of the crime scene. Morty, you may collect your things from the house whenever you wish. You are now free to go to Seattle with your father."

Isaac was anxious to get going. He was already into his second week away from work and he wanted to minimize the number of days he took off as much as possible. Since they were planning on driving to Seattle, he would probably be able to get to the office on Wednesday the fifteenth if they got on the road that day.

Morty and his father went to the house. Morty began gathering up his things and taking them out to his father's rental car. They had decided to drive to Seattle since it would be the easiest way to transport Morty's belongings to his father's house. It was only about a thirteen-hour drive, his father had said, but they were getting a late start and would have to stay the night somewhere in Oregon.

Morty's main concern was for the animals he kept in his aquarium and terrariums. In his aquarium, he had three bluegills, two green sunfish, and two black Crappies. He filled a couple of buckets he'd used to make water changes halfway with water from the tank, then he caught the fish and put them in the two buckets. The water level was low enough so that it wouldn't splash out in the car as long as they took care to drive slowly and smoothly. He also put the tiger Salamander and the red-legged frog he had been keeping in a small plastic container he had for the purpose of transporting such creatures along with half an inch of water. He planned to let the fish, and the amphibians go at a nearby lake. They were native species so they should have no trouble surviving and wouldn't cause havoc in the environment. Such considerations were important to Morty.

The alligator lizard, western skink, and the striped racer he caught and took out to the field behind the house and let them go. He drained the aquarium and cleaned things up a bit. The rest he left for the people his grandparents had hired to deal with. He was sad to see his menagerie dismantled, but it would be impossible to safely move the various species to Seattle without expending a great deal of time and money. He would just have to see what animals he could collect up there if his father would allow him to keep some in the apartment in which he lived. The prospect of the challenge of studying and capturing the species native to the Seattle area heartened him.

When he was finished packing up, he took one last long look at the house that had been his home for the first fifteen years of his life. It blew his mind to think how much his life had changed in a few short weeks. His mother was dead, he was no longer going to Livermore High School, and he was moving to Seattle to live with his father. And he had gold fever. It hadn't all really sunk in yet – as if he were in a state of shock. As they drove away and he watched the house recede in the distance, Morty was in a morose mood. After a while he shook himself out of it and started making plans for the future. When would he have an opportunity to get back to the Vasco Caves and conduct a thorough search for more gold?

On Tuesday, February 14th, Ian Seare got a phone call at the station from Jim Burt. Seare asked him to come in to answer a few questions about his role in Morty Schwartzkopf's transaction with Diablo Coins. He also asked him to bring the list of customers who had come to Diablo Coins on Friday, February 3rd that Fritz Utrecht had prepared for him.

When Jim Burt arrived at ten thirty and after they had exchanged the usual courtesies, Seare said to him, "I don't know how much Mr. Utrecht has told you about my conversation with him. I'm investigating the murder of Clarissa Phalen. You may have read about it in the papers."

"I don't often read the papers, but Fritz did mention that you had come to the shop and told me the gist of the nature of your questions."

"As I mentioned to him, it is standard procedure to establish the whereabouts of all persons with any connection to the victim, however remote, at the time the crime was committed."

"I understand, but I don't really see that I am connected to the victim in any way. I had never met the woman."

"No, but her son sold Diablo Coins a rare gold piece, and he told us that more such gold pieces were stolen from their home at the time of the murder."

"I see, I didn't know about that."

"Can you tell me where you were between the hours of ten and two that day?"

"Well, let's see. I figured you would ask me that since you asked Fritz. By the way, here is the information you asked Fritz to prepare." He took a folded sheet of paper from his jacket pocket and handed it to Seare. "That morning, I went over to the city to examine the coin collection in the estate of the late Mr. Harry Cooper. The collection is to be auctioned off next week, and we may be interested in purchasing certain items. I left Livermore at around eight thirty in the morning and didn't get back until around two thirty in the afternoon."

"So you headed to San Francisco at eight thirty and didn't return to Livermore until two thirty, is that correct?"

"Yes, but look here, Inspector, is all this really necessary? I can assure you that neither Fritz nor I had anything to do with that woman's death."

"Bear with me. You cannot, then, verify that Mr. Utrecht was in the coin shop between the hours of ten and two?"

"No, only that he was there when I returned at two thirty."

"I would like the name and phone number of the location where you examined the coin collection in San Francisco."

"No problem. I have already written it down for you." He handed over a file card.

"Thank you, Mr. Burt. That will be all for now."

"You're welcome," Jim Burt replied and he turned and walked out of the inspector's office.

There were nine names on the list of customers that Fritz Utrecht had supplied to Inspector Seare. Of those, six had visited the shop between the hours of ten and two. Seare had some of his men contact them and they were able to get hold of all six of them. All of them either knew Mr. Utrecht and confirmed that he was in the shop on February 3rd during the time period in question, or when given a description of Utrecht, confirmed that a man answering that description had helped them while they were in Diablo Coins at that time on that date. Fritz Utrecht's alibi seemed unshakeable.

A call to the executor of the estate of the late Harry Cooper confirmed that a coin dealer by the name of Jim Burt had come to examine and evaluate the coin collection on Friday the third of February, but that he had arrived at ten o'clock and left at eleven thirty. Seare contemplated that. Burt had been finished with his stated business in San Francisco at eleven thirty, but had not arrived back in Livermore until two thirty. Seare calculated the distance from San Francisco to Livermore at forty-five miles, so the drive would take forty-five minutes minimum perhaps longer depending on the traffic.

Jim Burt's alibi was not solid.

Seare picked up the telephone and called Diablo Coins to speak to Jim Burt. As luck would have it, he answered the phone. When Seare told him what he'd found out and asked him to account for his activities from eleven thirty to two thirty, Burt asked if he could speak to Seare in private and would it be all right if he came by the station after lunch. Seare said he could see him at one o'clock.

When Jim Burt arrived, he greeted Seare and sat down. He said, "It wasn't convenient for me to talk about this on the phone in the shop. Inspector, I'm a married man and it wouldn't do my marriage any good if my wife got wind of what I'm about to tell you." His expression was sheepish. "After I finished my business for our shop, I went to a massage parlor over on Sutter Street."

"Go on," was all Seare said.

"I was in there for over an hour, then I had lunch at Rick's Burgers on Van Ness. After that I drove back to Livermore. That's why I didn't get back here until two thirty. I had hoped to avoid telling you about that – as I say if my wife found out, she'd kill me."

"For getting a massage?"

"Well…"

"I see. Of course we'll need to corroborate that. What is the name of the business and the name of the masseuse?"

"It's called Madame Butterfly and I saw a girl who goes by the name of Suki."

"Had you ever been there before?"

"No."

"Did you meet anyone or interact with anyone at Rick's Burgers?"

"Just the waitress. I don't know if she'd remember me or if any of the other staff would."

"Did you happen to pay by credit card at either of these establishments?"

"No."

"All right, Mr. Burt. We'll check into that. Relax, there's no reason for us to speak to your wife about this, assuming it all checks out. We'll need a photo of you."

"If it'll help clear me I guess there's no help for it."

Seare got up from his desk, walked over and opened the door and called to one of his men, "Burkhart, get Sanchez over here with the Polaroid." Sanchez came with the camera and took a picture of Jim Burt. When he was finished Seare said, "All right, Mr. Burt, that'll be all," and Burt left with his head down.

After Jim Burt had departed, Seare called one of his men by the name of Terrence Teufel into his office and told him to close the door. When he had done so he said, "Listen, Teufel, I have a cookie of an assignment for you. You know the Phalen investigation? Well, Burt's alibi for the time the murder was committed turns out to be that he went to a massage parlor on Sutter Street in the city. A place called Madame Butterfly. Says he saw a girl called Suki. I want you to go over there and see her and see if she gave Burt a *massage* on Friday, February third around noon, got it?

"Sounds like the kind of establishment that gives massages with a happy ending," Terrence commented.

"Don't get any ideas, Teufel."

"I wouldn't dream of it, sir."

"You'd better call ahead and make an appointment just to make sure she'll be there. No sense in going all that way for nothing. Take this picture of Burt. Also stop by a burger joint on Van Ness called Rick's Burgers and see if any of the waitresses or employees remember him having lunch there that day at twelve thirty or thereabouts."

Teufel said, "Okay, boss."

Teufel was about five foot ten, slim, with black hair which he slicked back, brown eyes, a thin rather pointed nose and thin lips. He had a certain style – suave mannerisms. He was a smooth talker and quite the ladies' man to hear him tell it. He didn't fit the part of a police detective, which was why Seare had chosen him for the assignment. He thought the girl might be more likely to talk to him.

Teufel looked in the San Francisco Yellow Pages under massage parlors and found the address and phone number for Madame Butterfly on Sutter Street. He dialed the number and a woman answered, "Hello."

"I'd like to make an appointment with Suki."

"Suki off today."

"How about at eleven tomorrow morning?"

"Suki no work morning. How 'bou 'nother girl?"

"No, I want to see Suki. When will she be in tomorrow?"

"Two o'clock. You see Suki two o'clock, K?

"OK, tomorrow at two o'clock."

"Bye."

Terrence said, "Bye," but she had already hung up. He was not at all confident that he really had an appointment. He looked up the address of Rick's Burgers on Van Ness.

The next day Terrence Teufel left Livermore after lunch. The traffic on 580 West flowed smoothly all the way across the Bay Bridge and into the Tenderloin. That was a minor miracle in and of itself. He located Madame Butterfly on Sutter Street. It had a big pink sign hanging out perpendicularly high up above the sidewalk with 'Madame Butterfly' painted in large cursive red lettering, a drawing of a butterfly, and the word 'Massage' with a phone number down below. Terrence had to circle around several different blocks until he finally found a parking space he could barely squeeze into. He was about twenty minutes early. Should he go in hoping she'd be there or should he wait? He decided to wait. He spent most of the twenty minutes strolling around a couple of blocks, then headed back with a few minutes to spare.

Terrence pressed the doorbell and, when he heard a buzz and the heavy click of the electromagnet engaging, pulled open the heavy metal security door on the street and stepped inside. A long stairway covered by a worn out burgundy carpet led up to another security door with a small square curtained window in it at eye level. He climbed the stairs. There was another doorbell mounted on the right hand side and pushing it he heard a buzzing sound inside. In a few moments the curtain flashed open and closed again and the door was opened. A lovely, petite Asian girl wearing a flimsy, short, red, low cut dress with thin shoulder straps and silver leather thong sandals on her feet, the toenails of which were painted red, greeted him and, after he had stepped in, closed the door. She had an amazing rack that was surprisingly large for her petite frame. She had to have had a boob job. Terrence wanted to reach out and squeeze one of her breasts to confirm his hypothesis, but he resisted. She had a cute round face and short black hair that curved forward at her jaw line. He thought she was probably southeast Asian, perhaps Vietnamese. From a brightly lit hallway off to his right came the chatter of female voices in some indistinct foreign tongue. Terrence took a long look at the girl's cleavage, then shifting his gaze to her dark brown eyes he asked, "Is Suki here? I have a two o'clock appointment."

She said, "I Suki."

"Hi, Suki. I'm Terrence. Is there some place we can talk?"

"You wan' massa'? One howa, six'y dolla'."

"Look, Suki, I'm a police officer and I need to ask you some questions," he said, showing her his badge.

"Suki no do nutting wong, why you wan' ma'e me twubo."

"No, Suki. You're not in trouble," Terrence cooed soothingly, taking out the photo of Jim Burt. "I just need to ask you some questions about this man." He held up the photo for her to see.

"Come ove' heeah, si' dow'," she said grabbing him by the elbow and pulling him over to an alcove with several gaudy red velour upholstered armchairs near a window overlooking Sutter Street. She led him to one of the chairs and sat down opposite him in another. As he followed her, he observed a dark hallway leading off toward the back of the establishment opposite the lighted one. *That must be the way to the rooms where services are rendered*, he conjectured.

"You ma'e appoi'men'. You ta'e time, cos' me money," Suki admonished him, in a petulant voice.

"I know, I know. I'm sorry. I'm just doing my job." He held out the photo again and asked, "I need to know if you gave this man a massage about two weeks ago. Was he here on February third? That was a Friday."

"I no know, so many cusomers…" She took the photo from his hand and studied it. "I no know. He loo' familia'. Maybe I see him befo'e. I no shuh. If he come heeah I no rememba wha' day."

He took back the photo and said, "Okay, Suki, thank you for your time," and stood up. She stood up close to him. Rubbing her hand up and down the lapel of his sports jacket, and tilting her head to the side, she looked up at him and said in a sultry voice, "You han'some, you shuh you no wan' massa'?"

Terrence looked in her eyes and then down at her cleavage again. It sure was tempting. He said, "Suki, I'm a cop. Aren't you afraid I'd arrest you?"

"Me gi' you goo' massa'. One howa six'y dolla'. Why arres? Massa' no ieego."

"I'm sorry, Suki. I'm working. Here's twenty dollars for your time," he said taking a twenty out of his wallet and handing it to her.

"Phank you," Suki said and led him back to the door. She opened it and he went through and turning back he saw her smiling and waving her fingers through the half closed door. "Come ba' 'notha time," she purred. As he walked down the stairs he wondered how he could put that twenty on his expense account. He got halfway down the stairs when he decided what the hell, why not put that twenty to good use. He did an about-face, climbed the stairs again, and rang the bell.

Rick's Burgers was within walking distance on Van Ness. When Teufel got there he asked to speak to the manager. He scrutinized the interior of the burger joint. He read a large sign that proclaimed Rick's Burgers 'The Home of the Two Pound Burger'. Teufel observed the wall of fame under the sign that was covered with photographs of people who had successfully consumed one of Rick's two-pound burgers and won the Rick's Burger eating challenge. Black T-shirts with white lettering proclaiming 'I Conquered the Two Pound Burger at Rick's Burgers – San Francisco' were pinned up around the sign and were awarded to patrons who were actually able to devour the monster burger. *Only in America*, Terrence Teufel thought, shaking his head.

Teufel showed the manager the photo of Jim Burt and told him what he needed to know. Terrence asked him which waitresses were working on Friday, the 3rd of February. Fortunately, the same three waitresses who had been working on that Friday were working again that day. Unfortunately, none of them had any recollection of Jim Burt having eaten lunch there on that Friday almost two weeks ago, nor did any other employees or the manager.

On his way out, Teufel stopped to take a closer look at the photos on the wall of fame. There must've been a couple of hundred of them. Teufel did a double take when he thought he saw Jim Burt's photo there. He held the Polaroid up next to the photo on the wall. It sure looked like the same guy. Uncovering the bottom, he saw that indeed 'Jim Burt' was written there along with the date 'August 11, 1991'. So Jim Burt was a patron of Rick's Burgers, but there was still no evidence he'd been there on February 3rd. Jim Burt's alibi was as flimsy.

So the whole trip was a big washout and Jim Burt's alibi was as flimsy as ever.

Teufel drove back to Livermore and reported his findings, or lack thereof, to Seare, who commented, "Well, it was a couple of weeks ago and they all see a lot of customers. A massage parlor is a place where men want to remain anonymous. There'd be no paper trail unless he'd charged it, which he said he didn't do; same for the restaurant. So Jim Burt remains under suspicion."

"Do you suppose he's clever enough to think up a ruse like this knowing we couldn't verify it?"

"I wouldn't put it past him, but it's not going to help him much."

A few days later the case was put on the back burner for another home invasion murder and robbery had occurred on the other side of town.

II

December, 1997

On Monday, December 29th, Fritz Utrecht felt relaxed after the holiday weekend. Christmas had fallen on a Thursday that year, so he'd made a four-day holiday weekend out of it. He parked his Rolls Royce Phantom at the lot opposite his shop, jaywalked across the street, and unlocked the door of Diablo Coins. He almost never took a day off from his six-day-a-week routine, though he had to admit he appreciated the holidays on the calendar. He had spent the four-day weekend at his cabin at Lake Tahoe.

The alarm signal began beeping its strident warning as soon as he opened the door. Fritz flicked on the lights at the front of the shop and then waddled over to the wall-mounted keypad and punched in the alarm code. Then he went about his usual routine of removing the cloths with which he always covered the display cases before leaving each day so that their contents could not be seen through the storefront window. Of course, he kept his most valuable coins in a large safe in the back.

When he walked over to his desk and put his briefcase down on the floor, he thought he heard something.

Stopping in his tracks, he cocked his head and listened intently. Must have been his imagination he presumed. Then as he pulled his rolling desk chair back from his desk preparing to sit down, there it was again. He couldn't put his finger on it. It was a strange sort of vibration – rather like the sound of a Peruvian rain stick. It seemed to be emanating from under his desk.

Supporting himself with his right hand on the edge of the desk and his left on the seat of his chair, being mindful not to let the chair roll out from under his weight, he lowered his corpulence until he was down on his hands and knees and peered under the desk. Like lightning something lashed out and he felt a sharp prick and a shooting pain on the back of his right hand. He let out a shriek and jerked his hand back reflexively, falling on his left side against the chair. He scrambled backward frantically. *What the hell!* Something had bitten him – as improbable as it seemed to his addled brain he was fairly certain it was a snake.

He scurried down the hallway to the back of the shop and flipped on the hall light, which cast its glow under the desk. *My god!* It was a snake – a rattlesnake was coiled up under his desk, its head poised to strike again, the tip of its tail raised vertically behind its body shaking menacingly.

"Help! Help!" he screamed. He had to get to his phone – it was on his desk. He scampered past the side of his desk and around to the front as fast as his pudgy legs would carry him and snatching up the cordless handset, backpedaled to the front door all the while keeping his eyes on the space at the bottom of the desk. He couldn't see the snake from there. He jerked the door open and stepping outside in a panic he yanked it shut. He dialed 911. "Help! I've been bitten by snake! A rattlesnake! Send an ambulance!" Fritz screeched into the phone hysterically. His hand was tingling. It had turned black and blue and was beginning to swell up.

"Calm down, sir. What is your location?" the operator inquired placidly.

Calm down? Is she serious? Calm down! "Diablo Coins! Coin shop! Uh… four thirteen First Str…" Fritz Utrecht collapsed on the sidewalk, the phone falling from his hand and clattering on the concrete.

"Hello? Hello! Sir, are you still with me?"

***

Morty's life had taken a turn for the better since he'd moved to Seattle with his father. Living with his father, he had free rein and it was a great relief not to be under his mother's thumb. He had money to spend and was delighted with the independence he had once he turned sixteen and got his driver's license. True, he didn't have his own car, but Isaac would often let Morty borrow his car in the evenings when he got home from work and on weekends.

Isaac's real estate business had also picked up. He had a much more steady income than he had had in quite some time. He was happy to have Morty living with him and to have a chance to get to know his son well for the first time since his divorce from his mother. His ability to provide for Morty in their new life together helped to assuage the guilt he felt for not having been a part of his son's life for such a long time and for all the child support payments he'd missed over the years.

Shortly after their arrival, they had gone to Nova High School on Twentieth Avenue East to enroll Morty. Socially, the three years Morty spent at Nova were the best years of his life up to that point. By his junior year, his acne had begun to clear up and when Isaac's business became more solvent, he took Morty to an optometrist to have his eyes examined and get fitted for contact lenses. He fell in with a clique that was into grunge music and culture and had a group of friends to hang out with for the first time since he was in grade school.

Isaac hoped to strengthen the bond with his son by participating in some activity together. He had taken up knife throwing a few years back, and he thought Morty might enjoy it as well. The boy needed to get involved in some kind of manly activity, Isaac thought. It would toughen him up. Isaac thought Morty was a bit soft, ironically enough. He brought Morty to his knife and hawk-throwing club – The Seattle Slinger.

Morty took to the sport right from the start and showed considerable talent. Isaac gifted Morty a set of three small throwing knives in a sheath on a belt loop. Morty began throwing regularly. On hikes, he would wear the knives on his belt and whenever he encountered a suitable tree stump, he would practice throwing his knives into it. As the days wore on he developed into quite an accurate knife thrower.

During his junior year, Morty got a job working weekends at the Ebony Jungle Vivarium, which was a twenty-minute bus ride from their apartment. He enjoyed learning more about the various reptile and amphibian species they carried as well as scorpions and tarantulas. He was able to save most of the money he earned and was planning to buy a used car once he graduated. Morty had lost some credits when he'd transferred from Livermore High to Nova High in Seattle, and as a result, had to take an additional semester's worth of classes in order to meet the graduation requirements. Thus, he didn't graduate until December of 1997. He told his father he wanted to drive across the country after he finished high school, and visit all the famous aquariums he'd read about, like the Shedd Aquarium in Chicago, the Newport Aquarium in Kentucky, near Cincinnati, the New York Aquarium, and the National Aquarium in Baltimore. As the winter of '97 approached, he was meticulously planning the route he wanted to take and the cities he would visit.

***

Ian Seare had been kept busy investigating other murder cases for the past three years, but he hadn't given up on the Phalen murder. It wasn't a cold case – it was more of a cool case. After the incident involving Fritz Utrecht,

Sear'd spoken to Jim Burt asking him if he knew of any enemies who might have wanted Utrecht dead. Burt had said that there could potentially be quite a few people who might have sold coins to Diablo Coins and later learned, putting it euphemistically, that they hadn't gotten as good a deal as they'd thought they'd gotten at the time of the sale. It was the nature of the business. They were in it to make money after all. Seare asked if Ari Grunbergmight be one of those people. Yes, Burt had replied.

Seare recalled his investigation of Utrecht and Burt in the Phalen case. He remembered the day he'd stood in the doorway of Morty Schwartzkopf's room in the ransacked house as the kid packed up some of his clothes – how it had struck him as curious that virtually the only undisturbed items in the house were the kid's aquarium and terrariums. The kid had kept a snake. Not a rattlesnake, it's true – Schwartzkopf had told him it was a whipsnake at the time when he'd inquired about his animals – but a snake nevertheless. The kid was into snakes.

On a hunch he made a call to the Homicide Unit of the Seattle Police Department and spoke to an Inspector Lee. Seare gave him a brief synopsis of the Phalen case including a detailed description of the 1850 Baldwin and Company ten dollar gold coin. He said he'd fax him a photo and description of the coin. He requested a list of coin dealers in the Seattle area and asked Lee to contact him if there should be any notoriety surrounding the sale of such coins in the area.

Two days later, Lee called back to inform Seare that just over two weeks before, on Saturday, December 13th, a Seattle coin dealer by the name of Northwest Rare Coins and Bullion had auctioned off two of the extremely rare 1850 Baldwin and Company ten dollar gold pieces to an anonymous buyer for two hundred and thirty-five thousand dollars. The seller had also remained anonymous. It had caused quite a stir.

After Ian Seare hung up, he reflected. Two rare coins of the exact same type as the one Ari Grunberghad sold. Auctioned off by a coin dealer in Seattle. It had to be him. It was too great a coincidence to be anyone else. So Ari Grunberghad been lying when he'd told Seare and his men that the coins he'd found had been stolen. Seare went over the case file again with the assumption that pretty much everything Ari Grunberghad told them was a lie. He upbraided himself for not taking that approach right from the start. Was it the boy's youth that had led him astray? Without the robbery motive in the murder of Clarrisa Phalen, the spotlight was now squarely trained upon young Mortimer Schwarzkopf.

On the morning of December 30th, Seare called Isaac Grunberg and asked to speak to Morty. When Isaac said Morty wasn't there, Seare asked him about Morty's whereabouts. Isaac said that Morty was on a cross-country driving trip. When asked when he had left Seattle, Isaac replied that it had been on the morning of December 23rd. When Ian Seare expressed surprise that Morty would leave on a trip two days before Christmas, Isaac explained that they didn't celebrate Christmas. Isaac said that he'd had a call from Morty from Chicago and that he'd said he was having a great time. He'd told Isaac all about visiting the Shedd Aquarium. Morty was intent on visiting many of the well-known aquariums in the U.S. on the trip. He loved aquariums.

When Seare asked what make and model car Morty was driving and what the license plate number was, Isaac inquired why that was significant. Seare told him about the incident with Fritz Utrecht, the coin dealer to whom Morty had sold a gold coin back in January of '95, and the recent sale of two of the same type of rare gold coins in Seattle. Isaac said he was sure that neither of those events had anything to do with his son and that in any case he couldn't be involved since he was halfway across the country at the time of the incident. When pressed he told Seare that he had helped Morty buy a used '86 Honda Accord on December 20th. It was a light brown two-door sedan with Washington plates and the license number was Y539771. Lastly, Seare had asked Isaac Grunberg if Morty's appearance had changed in any way in the last three years and Isaac told him about the contacts. Seare thanked Mr. Schwartzkopf saying that he was probably right – that his son was not involved.

Seare put out an APB on the car immediately. If Ari Grunberghad been involved in the presumed attack on Fritz Utrecht, he might still be in the area. Seare had his men check the guest registrations at all of the area hotels and motels in the cities of Livermore, Dublin, and

Pleasanton to see if a Ari Grunbergor any young man approximately eighteen years of age answering his description and driving an '86 Accord with Washington license plate number Y539771 had registered there.

***

Morty had taken pains to keep off the radar since moving to Washington with his father. He had kept his wad of money and the two gold coins well hidden from his dad. He spent the money sparingly and resisted the temptation to sell any more coins. He planned to revisit the site where he'd found the coins to see if there were any more buried there; he just didn't know when he would be able to get back down to California. Gradually he developed a plan to buy a car after he graduated from Nova High and make a road trip to Northern California. He got a job and made a show of saving money so as to make it plausible that he could afford to purchase a car. He would ask his father for a little help and planned to spend no more than fifteen hundred on it to make it seem affordable to him.

In order to bamboozle his father into thinking he was planning to drive cross-country, Morty made a show of making elaborate plans for visiting well-known aquariums back east. He father was enthusiastic about Morty's plans, regaling him with stories of cross-country road trips he had made when he was a young man. Isaac did question the wisdom of embarking on a cross-country driving trip in the wintertime. He argued that it would be better to wait until summertime when the road conditions would be less hazardous, but Morty wouldn't hear of it.

In his senior year, one of his friends at school, who made money by helping kids get fake IDs, helped Morty obtain one in the name of Troy Blackhead. He forged a fictitious out-of-state birth certificate, utility bills, and other documents that established residency and stated that his birthday was on February 17th 1976, which made him out to be over twenty-one. That was not so implausible since Morty was six four by then. Morty took the documents to the Department of Licensing to apply for a genuine fake Washington driver's license. He passed the written test and driving test and a few weeks later, he was in business. Morty used the ID to buy alcohol for himself and his friends, which made him a popular guy with whom to hang out and a regular at parties.

After Morty had graduated and was on the point of embarking upon his trip, he needed more money to carry out his plans, so he decided it was time to test the waters in the coin market for selling the other two coins. He was flabbergasted when the two coins he took to a Seattle coin dealer were auctioned off for two hundred and thirty-five thousand dollars. He was also livid about having been cheated by Fritz Utrecht when he had sold him one of the coins three years before. He vowed to teach Utrecht a lesson he'd never forget.

Even though he was then big time flush with cash, he asked his father to pitch in a few hundred dollars for an '86 Accord advertised in the paper. He also searched for a garage he could rent and when he found one that suited his purpose, he paid a year's rent in advance. On the day of his departure from Seattle, after a heartfelt goodbye with his dad, Morty drove to the garage he'd rented. He parked the Accord in the garage, then took a bus over to a car dealership where he bought a brand new loaded black Jeep Grand Cherokee – a vehicle he'd long coveted. The salesman raised his eyebrows when Morty paid in cash and asked to see some identification. Morty had them put in a car alarm. After that Morty drove over to the garage to get his bags and gear. He transferred them from the Honda to the Jeep, then closed the garage and locked it. It was past eight by the time he got on the road. As he drove down the freeway in the gathering gloom, Morty felt freer than he'd ever felt in his life before.

As Morty drove through Oregon the following day, he grew concerned about the fact that there were no license plates on the Jeep. He thought a cop might be more likely to pull him over since he had no plates. He thought he could steal some plates off a car and put them on his Jeep. He concluded that since he was heading to California, it would be best to wait until he got there and steal some California plates so he would blend in better while there. He stopped at a hardware store to pick up a set of wrenches.

When Morty got to Northern California, he stopped to rest in a town called Weed. He definitely would have to smoke some weed in honor of his arrival in Weed. Late that night he started scouting for a set of California plates to put on the Jeep. It was tricky since he had no plates of his own to exchange for the ones he would steal. The owner might not notice for a while if the plates on his car were not his own, but he surely would notice if his car had no plates at all. At first he tried to find a vehicle that looked like it was seldom used – perhaps one that was kept under a cover in a driveway. When he couldn't find anything to fit the bill, he decided on a different expedient. He would play a little game of musical license plates. It was risky because it would take a while to accomplish and would greatly increase the chances he'd be seen removing the plates.

He located a car parked in a dark spot on a driveway, stole over with the wrench he'd determined to be the right size and removed the plates. Then he drove some blocks away until he found another car parked in a favorable place and removed its plates, putting the plates from the first car in their place. Lastly he drove to a deserted street in a warehouse district and put the second car's plates on his Jeep. He hoped that would throw them off, but he thought he'd better be moving on. He rolled a joint and lit it up once he was back on Interstate five heading south. So much for Weed. Morty ended up smoking weed in honor of his departure from Weed and his successful acquisition of California license plates.

When Morty arrived in the Bay Area, he went shopping to pick up a few items he'd need. He stopped by a restaurant supply warehouse just off the eight eighty freeway in Oakland to buy two clear storage containers with tight fitting lids – an eight quart one and a twenty-two quart one. As he was passing through Castro Valley on his way out to Livermore, he swung by Phil's Hardware and a CBS Pharmacy to purchase some medical tape, duct tape, cotton balls, rubber bands, construction paper, straws, and string. Lastly, Morty went to a pet store just off the boulevard to buy a cat toy. It was one of those spherical plastic mesh toys about the size of a golf ball with a bell inside. With these items and a couple that he'd gotten at Ebony Jungle Vivarium back in Seattle before he'd quit his job in early December, he was ready to carry out the next phase of his plan.

The following morning Morty left the Motel Thirty-Seven in Livermore at which he was staying and went straight to a barbershop. He told the barber to cut it all off. When the barber asked if he also wanted a shave, he declined. Leaving the barbershop, he put on his Mariners cap and drove out to the spot where he used to leave his bike when he went hiking at the Vasco Caves. When he got out there he was met by a rude surprise. A fence had been put up and a sign posted stating that the area was now the 'Vasco Caves Regional Preserve', a part of the East Bay Regional Park District. It went on to say that, in order to protect the preserve's unique resources, public access was limited to guided tours only. There was a phone number to call for reservations.

That's a hell of a note, Morty thought to himself. *I've been coming here since I was a kid and I've always respected the place. Who the hell are they to tell me I can't go there anymore except by making a reservation for some namby-pamby guided tour*. He was royally pissed off. He had to get in there at some point, but for the time being it was best to back off and assess the situation.

Morty drove back down Vasco Road and on over to Laughlin Road to get to the place from which he used to hike up to Brushy Peak. When he got there, *Damn! More fences and more signs!* This time the signs proclaimed the 'Brushy Peak Regional Preserve'. There was a parking lot near a house and a barn. He saw a signboard with postings of a map and park rules. As Morty got out of his car a couple pit bulls in the fenced yard of the house started barking at him furiously. Morty was fuming as he read the rules. At least he was allowed to hike here without making a reservation, but as he studied the map of the park he saw that the upper reaches of Brushy Peak itself were off limits. He got back into his car to mull things over, wishing the damn dogs would shut the hell up.

This development had really put a crimp in Morty's plans. He knew the best place to go to find rattlesnakes, but it was now in The Vasco Cave Preserve. He might be able to find one in the Brushy Peak Preserve, but collecting wasn't allowed so there was the risk of getting in hot water over it. He tried to think of another place where he might get what he'd come for, but every place that came to mind was now either park land or private property. Looking around, there was no one in sight. There were a couple of other cars in the lot. He decided he'd encounter more of the same difficulties elsewhere, so it might as well be here.

Morty got out of his car and went around and opened up the back. He had on a baggy long-sleeved shirt, baggy pants, and his hiking boots. He loaded his backpack with the eight-quart storage container that he had wrapped in black construction paper, his five foot collapsible snake stick, his snake handling gloves, a roll of duct tape, and a quart bottle of water. He strapped his snake tongs to the side of his pack. After locking the car, he put on his aviator sunglasses and set out. The pits continued barking incessantly and gravitated to the corner of their yard near the gate to the hiking trail as Morty went through it. He was glad when he had gotten out of sight around a bend and could no longer hear them.

That day Morty did not encounter any snakes of any kind. At least he was able to scout out the lay of the land. He stuck to what was called the Brushy Peak Loop Trail which passed east-west along the slopes of Brushy Peak just over three hundred feet below the summit at its closest point. He only met a couple of middle-aged women who came up behind him chatting non-stop, to Morty's annoyance, and a grizzled bearded fellow who also carried a backpack. He scouted out a few places where he could slip off the trail and head higher up Brushy Peak without being seen as long as no one was in sight on the trail when he left it.

On his third day of hiking around the slopes of Brushy Peak, Morty found what he'd been seeking. He had departed the trail at the same point the past two days and made his way up and around the peak near the top. The old trails were still visible and as he followed one around a sandstone formation that was pocked with pigeon holes on its western face like the wall of an old post office sorting room, there it was. Smack in the middle of a sunny stretch of the trail, about fifteen feet ahead was coiled a western rattlesnake. Morty stopped in his tracks. The rattler looked to be four or five feet long, which suited his purpose well.

Slowly stepping back behind the post office rock, he took off his backpack and leaned it up against the rock. Opening it, he took out the gloves, the snake stick, and the storage container. He unstrapped the snake tongs from the side of the pack. Carrying these things he peeked around the rock, then crept forward stealthily. This was where the snake handling skills he'd picked up at the Ebony Jungle would stand him in good stead.

Morty stole to within seven feet of the serpent. He knew that the maximum length of a western rattlesnake was approximately five feet and that since the length of a rattler's strike is about half its body length, the maximum length of this snake's strike would be about two and a half feet. The snake was aware of his presence, facing him and continuously flicking out its tongue. It was coiled in a sort of figure eight with its head raised and tail up behind, but it wasn't shaking its rattle as of yet.

Morty slowly set down his equipment. He picked up his collapsible snake stick and extended it to its five-foot length. Picking up the storage container, he took off the lid. This was going to be tricky for the container was rather small for a snake of this size, but it was the biggest container he could conceal in his pack. Gently standing the container on the ground in front of him, he reached back and wedged the edge of lid inside the top of the back of his pants. He would have to be quick with it. He put on his snake handling gloves. Using the snake stick, Morty pushed the container closer to the rattler very slowly. The plastic made a scraping sound as it slid across the dry ground which was unfortunate but couldn't be helped. When he had the container about three feet from the snake and off to the right a bit, the snake emitted its first rattle. Morty withdrew the snake stick and transferred it to his left hand then he picked up the snake tongs with his right. Now came the moment of truth. Morty had to manipulate the rattlesnake into the container and get the lid securely on without getting bitten.

The key was to grab the snake's body with the tongs about one third of the way down from its head. The snake tongs were only forty inches long, however, so it wouldn't be easy. Morty had wrapped the jaws of the tongs with foam padding and taped it in place to make sure not to injure the snake. He needed this snake alive and well. As Morty reached out with the snake stick within a foot of the rattler its tail began to vibrate vigorously, emitting the characteristic rattle for which they are named. Despite the fact that Morty was expecting it, the rattler's strike was so quick and violent that he instinctively jumped. The snake had recoiled almost as quickly. The second time the snake struck, Morty got the stick in on its body right after it recoiled, sliding it under the snake and turning the hook upward. He lifted it up but it slid off and began to slither to the left. Morty brought snake stick down on it, pinning it down too hard. He was afraid he'd injured it, but swooped in with the jaws on the snake tongs open and grabbed the rattler in the middle of its body. Morty swiftly lifted the snake and swung it over the container. The snake thrashed and writhed. As he pushed the tongs down into the container, it fell on its side. He manipulated the snake's head into the opening of the container. The darkness of the black construction paper wrapped container appeared to offer a refuge to the snake. Morty let go with the tongs. The front quarter of the snake was in the container.

Morty quickly pulled out the lid and dropping to his knees he clapped the lid over the opening of the container, trapping the remainder of the snake's body between the edge of the lid and the rim of the container. Righting it, he loosened the lid and grasping the snake's body, he thrust it further into the container. The snake lashed out, its head striking against the lid. Morty shook the container and the end of the tail slid through the gap. Morty pushed the lid home firmly and then sat back breathing heavily.

Looking at the large snake in the relatively small container concerned Morty. It was then that he realized that he should have somehow made a hole in the lid so the snake could breathe. He wasn't sure whether or not it would have enough air during the hike back to his car. He would just have to stop every once in awhile and crack the lid open a little to let in some fresh air – something he would rather have avoided. Just to make absolutely sure that the lid would not come off in his backpack while he hiked, Morty duct taped it down tightly.

By the time Morty got back to his motel room, he was exhausted. The adrenaline rush he'd gotten from his struggle with the rattlesnake had worn off, leaving him drained and listless. He still had to transfer the serpent into the larger storage container he'd bought and he wasn't looking forward to it. He wondered if he could make some holes in the hard plastic lid with the awl of his Swiss Army knife without cracking it. He gave it a try, turning the tip of the awl back and forth and removing bits of the plastic without putting too much pressure on the lid. It took him some time but he finally had a small hole in the top with only a few half-inch cracks branching out from it. In another twenty minutes he had three more holes in the lid for a total of four. That would have to do. A piece of duct tape on each should serve to plug them when the time came.

Morty figured the best way to transfer the snake would be to yank open the lid of the small container while holding it upside down and dump the snake into the large container, then clap the top on as quickly as possible. He breathed a huge sigh of relief when it came off without a hitch. Duct taping the lid down, he left the snake in his motel room and went out to get something to eat. He had some time to kill before his midnight excursion.

At around midnight, Morty began making his preparations. Using the blade of his Swiss Army knife he carefully cut the cat toy in half at the seam around its equator. He removed the bell and putting a cotton ball in its place, he used the surgical tape to tape the two halves together again at the seam where he'd cut them apart. He set it aside next to the bottle of Halothane that he had filched from The Ebony Jungle Vivarium shortly before he quit working there. Next he opened the bag of rubber bands of assorted sizes and chose one he thought would fit snugly around the rattlesnake's head without being too tight. Taking the ball of string, he cut off a length equivalent to his arm span. He tied one end of the string tightly around a spot on the rubber band. Morty tore off four two-inch lengths of duct tape and covered the holes he'd made in the lid of the large storage container with them making sure no gases could escape. Opening the package of straws, he put a couple of them in his pack.

Halothane is an inhalation anesthetic. At the Ebony Jungle Vivarium Morty had seen how they occasionally used it when working with or transporting large, dangerous snakes. He had read about its use during surgery on endangered snakes for the purpose of implanting radio transmitters in order to track the snakes' movements.

Morty opened the window of his motel room but kept the curtains closed. He removed the duct tape he'd used to secure the lid of the container and unscrewed the top of the bottle of Halothane. After putting on his snake handling gloves, he doused the cotton ball inside the modified cat toy with Halothane, then quickly popped open the edge of the lid enough to drop the cat toy inside. The snake struck his gloved hand through the gap, making Morty flinch and jerk his hand away, but it was unable to penetrate the glove with its fangs. Shaken Morty clumsily shoved the lid back, trapping the snake's head between the lid and the lip of the container. He pulled it back and thrust the cat toy in as the snake fell back down then clapped the lid closed and pushed it down tightly. Breathing rapidly and feeling a bit faint, Morty looked in at the snake. It seemed to be all right. He wound a long strip of duct tape around the edge of the lid where it met the lip of the container to make sure it was airtight. It would take at least twenty minutes to knockout the rattler.

Morty gathered up the things he'd prepared and moved them to the door. He went out and opened the back of the Jeep. Looking around he saw no one about so he grabbed up the container and put it in the car. He got the rest of the things and put them in the back as well, then closed the motel room window and locked the door. He drove over to First Street and parked the Jeep in front of the business just past Diablo Coins – a dry cleaning establishment. It was now almost one a.m.

Climbing into the back of the Jeep, Morty used his flashlight to check on the snake. It had almost been twenty minutes. The rattler looked to be under. Morty lifted and tilted the container, rotating it gently in an attempt to maneuver the snake onto its back. An alert snake would exhibit a righting response when on its back and turn itself over onto its belly. If the snake lay on its back like a limp rope it was well under anesthesia for sure. Unfortunately, Morty couldn't quite get the snake on its back without flipping it harshly. He waited a while longer, then removing the duct tape from around the top, he put on his gloves and popped open the edge of the lid.

Extending his snake stick to only two feet long, Morty reached in the container with it and prodded the rattler. He flipped it on its back with some difficulty. No response. *Here goes nothing*, he thought to himself. Completely removing the lid and setting it down, Morty cautiously reached his gloved left hand in and gently picked up the rattlesnake by the base of its head. It was out cold. He slipped the rubber band with the string tied to it over its head and back to the base of its neck. It was time to revive the snake a bit to make sure it would recover.

Morty gently opened the rattler's mouth. Under the anesthesia, its fangs were retracted, but as soon as it recovered they would be protracted and the snake would thrash about, so Morty was walking a fine line and had to judge the degree of the rattler's recovery just right. Holding the head of the snake in the beam of the flashlight and using a straw as a ventilation tube, he placed it against the snake's trachea, just above its tongue and gently blew into its lung. Morty had observed this a few times at the vivarium but never on a rattlesnake. He tried to observe the snake's sides to see them rising, as he remembered you were supposed to do, but it was difficult in the poor light cast by the flashlight. After each gentle puff, he let the snake exhale. He could smell Halothane escaping the snake's lung and it made him woozy.

He watched the tail for signs the muscles were recovering. After just a few rounds of puffs and exhalations Morty observed signs of recovery, which wasn't surprising since the snake hadn't been under for long. The rattler suddenly gave a violent shake and Morty nearly lost his grip on it. It was time. He slipped the rubber band forward around the snake's mouth so as to keep it closed, then extinguishing the flashlight, he looked out the windows of the car. He'd been so absorbed in what he was doing he hadn't kept a proper lookout, but the street was deserted.

Carrying the snake, Morty got out of his car and swiftly strode over to the door of Diablo Coins. Kneeling down, he poked the tail of the rattler into the mail slot and slowly fed its body into the slot. As he came to the head, he took hold of the string and letting go of the head, he gently lowered the snake to the floor inside the shop. Finally, Morty gently tugged on the string through the slot, working the rubber band off the rattlesnake's head. In doing so, he had lifted the anterior third of the snake off the floor and when the snake thrashed violently again the rubber band came off. Holding the slot open with his finger, Morty pulled out the string and rubber band and stood up. He looked around. He looked through the window of the door. The snake was moving sluggishly. Morty was fairly sure it would be well recovered by morning. He got in his car and as he drove away he thought to himself that that would make for a nice, well-deserved present for Mr. Fritz Utrecht when he came to work in the morning. *Merry Christmas and a happy New Year!*

Morty slept in. He was exhausted from his activities of the night. He would have liked to have watched the coin shop as Fritz Utrecht came to work that morning to see the result of his stratagem for taking revenge on Utrecht for cheating him out of over a hundred thousand dollars, but he knew it was a bad idea. Instead he'd keep an eye on the local papers while he remained in town, which he hoped would not be for long.

He drove over to a shop named Gold Seekers in Concord that he'd found in the Yellow Pages. They sold a large line of metal detectors and he would need one for his quest that night. He chose the model that best fit his criteria of an excellent metal detector of lightweight, compact design. He wished that there was a collapsible model that could fit in his backpack, but he had to settle for the smallest, lightest one that was still a good machine.

Morty spent the rest of the day driving to the top of Mount Diablo and doing a little light hiking up there. He didn't want to do anything too strenuous for he would need to be well rested for the activity he had planned for that night. He hiked out to the Devil's Pulpit and scrambled up to the top. He sat down and ate the lunch he'd bought at a deli while enjoying the view out over Los Vaqueros Reservoir, Discovery Bay, and the Sacramento-San Joaquin River Delta to the slopes of the Sierras.

At around nine thirty that night Morty parked his Jeep at a pullout off Vasco Road from which he could hike out to the area of the Vasco Caves where he'd discovered the gold coins. He took his daypack loaded with his refillable quart water bottle, a bag of packaged trail mix and some beef jerky he'd bought at the deli earlier that day, a flashlight, and the military surplus shovel with its handle sticking out the top through the zipper, and dropped it over the fence. He tied a length of string onto the metal detector and gently lowered it over the fence as well. He put on his jacket for the night air was getting a bit chilly, locked his car, and climbed over the fence. He got out his flashlight. If they were going to try to keep him from visiting his favorite retreat and thwart his plans, he would just have to do it by stealth.

It was a clear night with a waning gibbous moon that helped light Morty's way over the rugged landscape and through the unique sandstone formations. He picked his way along northeast to the more familiar ground near where he used to stash his bike to hike up to the caves. Once he came upon the path he knew so well it was much easier. He knew the ground like the contours of his own face in a mirror. He believed he could navigate it even on a much darker night, but with the moon casting its luminance on the landscape, he made good time and reached the spot where he'd discovered the coins some three years earlier in under half an hour.

Morty set down the metal detector and taking off his pack and opening it, he removed the shovel. Taking up the metal detector he fiddled with the controls. He'd had the saleswoman demonstrate its use and had read the manual that came with it thoroughly. It was fairly straightforward.

Morty had read in *Treasure Hunter Magazine* that when you make a find, you should always dig deeper to see if there is more treasure below. He figured that it was possible that the coins he'd found were only a teaser of the mother lode, so to speak, and he was tingling with excitement as he began his search. Morty imagined himself like the Count of Monte Cristo with inexhaustible wealth and thereby supreme power over his destiny. He'd had a taste of it and he wanted more.

First he swept the area where the washout that had exposed the coins had occurred, but it was a washout – nothing more. He decided to scan the ground around the base of the phallic rock formation. It was a distinctive landmark, and he thought that if he were going to bury treasure, he would bury it in the vicinity of a just such a landmark to make it easy to locate when the time came to dig it up. He wondered who would have buried their gold way out there and why. Why hadn't they returned to retrieve it?

Half an hour of going over the ground around the phallus in concentric circles of ever increasing circumference left him frustrated, however. Was the metal detector even working? He needed something to test it on – his stainless steel water bottle. As he swept the metal detector over the bottle, it emitted a strident tone and a red light lit up. He adjusted the sensitivity knob to see how it affected the response. It was working all right. He walked back to where he'd been before and sat down on a rock. He shone his flashlight on the surrounding landscape. Where should he search? Perhaps this was all a wild goose chase. He thought about giving it up as a bad case of gold fever. It was cold and he was tired.

After resting for a bit Morty decided to try for a while longer – after all he'd come all this way and he shouldn't leave until he felt certain it was all in vain. As he shoved off the rock to get up he thought he felt it rock a little. He stood up on it and rocked his weight from side to side. It was slightly loose. He had an inkling that there might be something under it. Leaning into it from the uphill side he was able to rock it more. It was about the size of an ottoman and rather shaped like one too with a flat top that made a good seat. It was much too heavy to lift, but he thought he might be able to tumble it down the washout if he could get enough leverage to get it out of the hole in which the bottom half was buried.

Taking up the shovel he began to dig out the earth all around it, especially on the downhill side nearest the washout. When he thought it might do, he positioned himself on the uphill side and bracing his feet, he pushed with all his might. He'd get it up a few inches only to have it drop back into place as his strength waned. He was about to dig some more when he had the idea of wedging something under it when he had it raised. He used his flashlight to search for a log or something to use as a lever or to brace it. He wished he had brought a saw so he could saw off a branch of a tree. He thought the shovel might work as a lever, but he was concerned he might break it. He might need it to dig some more. There had to be something he could use. He thought about his water bottle. It was a stainless steel, quart bottle about three and a half inches in diameter. He might be able to get it wedged in the opening so as to allow him to push the rock again from a raised position. It was worth a try – the worst it could do was to dent the water bottle.

Getting it from his pack, he set the bottom of it at the base of the rock so he could shove it underneath as he lifted the rock. As he shoved the rock with his hands he tried to release one hand to shove the bottle under, but when he did so the rock slipped back down too far to get the bottle under. Then he tried putting his back to the rock and shoving with his feet and he was just able to get the bottle under. Turning around he shoved with his hands again. The gap was now twice as great and he reached the critical point of balance. With a last great heave the ground below gave way slightly and he pushed the rock over. It tumbled over and then slid a few feet down the gentle slope of the washout.

Morty snatched up the flashlight and shone it in the hole. It was just a dark earth hole. He got the metal detector and turning it on he swept the area where the rock had been. It immediately emitted a strong beep of a different tone than the one before and the red light lit up. Setting the metal detector down, Morty picked up the shovel and began to dig. It was hard to dig with a shovel that had such a short handle.

When he'd fully excavated the hole to an additional depth of six inches he took a breather. He took a good long drink of water from the dented bottle. When he had dug out the middle of the hole another six inches or so, he jabbed the shovel in again and he struck something. He shone the light on it. Wiping away some of the earth around the object he perceived what appeared to be a piece of leather. His excitement grew to a fever pitch. Using the shovel he spent another ten minutes frantically digging around the object until he had a section of it a foot long and three inches wide cleared to a depth of six inches. He could just get his fingers around the edges at the ends and taking a good grip, he yanked upward. It came up a bit and by yanking again a few more times a kind of flap came up from one side. Even in the moonlight he could see the reflection of light off the coins.

A wide smile lit up his face and he was so elated he had to shake his head to convince himself it was really true. He shone the flashlight on the gold and it gleamed brightly in the beam. He stuck his fingers in it and grabbed up a handful of the gold pieces, letting them fall from his hand back into the pile with heavy metallic clinking sounds. Some of the coins were like the ones he'd found before, but there were some large octagonal shaped ingots as well. It was all he could do to suppress a whoop, but he did because he immediately grew wary and afraid someone might discover him, as illogical as it seemed in such a relatively desolate place in the middle of the night.

He decided he should hurry now. He got his pack and started scooping up the coins and ingots and stuffing them in it. He had filled the small front compartment and the larger front compartment and part of the bottom of the largest compartment by the time he emptied what he presumed was some kind of leather bag. He tugged on the bag but the flap tore off. He got the metal detector and swept it over the hole again but it didn't react. *That must be all of it*, he thought, but it was plenty. He was rich beyond his wildest dreams.

Resting, he drank some more water. He was so charged with adrenaline that he didn't even feel tired. He just kept shaking his head in disbelief with a giant grin plastered on his face and his mouth agape. It was time to get going. He put his water bottle in the pack and closed it up. He would need the flashlight and he would have to carry the shovel and the metal detector. When he tried to lift the pack it was heavy as hell. He realized it was going to be a long hard trip back to his car with such a heavy load and immediately jettisoned the shovel and the metal detector. He could buy a thousand shovels and metal detectors. It would not do to be burdened by them now. Carrying the flashlight in his hand, he set out. After a few yards he turned and surveyed the scene of his greatest triumph for a few moments. His fingerprints were on the shovel and the metal detector. Would that matter? Sooner or later someone would find them and maybe they could be used to trace him. Someone might try to make a claim on his gold. He took off the pack and set it down. He took off his jacket and his sweatshirt and T-shirt. Using his T-shirt, he carefully wiped down the shovel and the metal detector and set them back down. He suddenly realized how cold he was. He put his T-shirt, sweatshirt and jacket back on, picked up his pack and surveyed the scene again. When he was satisfied that he hadn't left any clues, he set off down the path by which he had come. Glancing at his watch he saw that it was almost twelve thirty.

As Morty trudged back to his car, weighed down by his heavy, precious load, his mind was filled with thoughts of the fabulous future that lay ahead of him. He dreamed of all the things he'd buy and the women he'd have eating out of his hand for the first time in his life. He wouldn't have to go to college or work. He'd buy a big house with a swimming pool and party with his friends all day and night. He'd buy a case of liquor, a pound of herb, a state-of-the-art entertainment system, a fleet of jet skis, and drive a Ferrari... the list of material goods Morty desired was endless.

***

Shortly after midnight on Tuesday the 7th of July, Inspector Ian Seare was awoken by a call from one of his fellow detectives – Detective Terrence Teufel. After apologizing for disturbing the inspector in the middle of the night, he informed Seare that around midnight a Contra Costa Sheriff had found a brand new black Jeep Grand Cherokee parked in a pullout off Vasco Road. There didn't appear to be anything amiss with the vehicle and the sheriff suspected that the driver was on foot in the vicinity. The California plates on the vehicle were registered to a 1995 Buick Regal whose owner lived in Weed in northern California. A check of the vehicle identification number showed that the Jeep had been purchased at a dealership in Seattle, Washington on December twentieth and that the temporary registration was in the name of a Troy Blakeleyof Seattle. A Troy Blakeleyhad been issued a Washington driver's license some months before, however the address given proved to be that of a coffee shop in the University District. Since they had issued an APB for a Honda Accord with Washington plates driven by Ari Grunbergof Seattle, the deputy had thought there might be a connection.

Seare thanked him, saying that he'd done the right thing and he appreciated the deputy for having notified him. He told the deputy to get a fingerprint technician on the scene right away. After noting down the precise location of the vehicle, Seare hung up.

Grumbling about the travails of being a homicide inspector, Ian Seare got dressed and headed out the door. By the time he got to the scene, the backup for which the sheriff had called had arrived and they had opened the vehicle, disarmed the alarm, and searched it. Seare filled the sheriffs in on his investigation into the apparent attempt on Fritz Utrecht's life and the murder of Clarissa Phalen of Livermore in December of 1994.

The sheriffs showed Seare what they'd found in the vehicle: a Mariners' baseball cap, a collapsible wand-like instrument with a hook on one end, a yard-long device with jaws for gripping that had been wrapped with foam on one end and a trigger like grip on the other for opening and closing them, a length of string with a rubber band tied on one end, and a bottle of some chemical known as Halothane, which the label indicated was an inhalation anesthetic. The only significant document in the vehicle was the temporary registration in the name of Troy Blakeleythat had been taped onto the inside lower right-hand corner of the windshield.

The fingerprint technician had arrived, dusted for prints, and using his laptop, compared the primary prints found in the vehicle to those on file for one Mortimer Schwartzkopf. He confirmed that the prints were indeed Schwartzkopf's. Detective Teufel had arrived and he went over the car again himself.

A manhunt was organized. Schwartzkopf apparently had some clandestine business in the hills off Vasco Road. Seare recalled the young man's story of finding the gold pieces and how he'd made Schwartzkopf take him to the location on Brushy Peak to test the veracity of his claims. It had been obvious to him that the kid was lying about the location at the time. He'd stood in a defensive posture with his arms folded across his chest and wouldn't make eye contact for more than a moment as he told his tale. When Seare had pressed him after the strenuous hike up the mountain, he'd gotten flushed and grew faint from the stress. Telltale signs of a liar. Perhaps somewhere in the Vasco Caves area was the real location, and he'd felt compelled to return there – undoubtedly in the hope of finding more gold.

It was almost three when the bloodhound tracking team consisting of eight officers and four dogs arrived on the scene. They set the dogs on Morty's scent using the ball cap they'd found in the vehicle. The dogs immediately went to the spot at the fence on the eastern side of the road where Morty had clambered over it some hours earlier. The officers cut a gap in the fence line and letting the dogs through it, they were off on Morty's trail.

***

As Morty came around a twenty-foot high rock outcropping in a state of ecstasy he looked toward where he'd left his car to the southwest and stopped short. He could see the headlights of a car stopped near his and someone was shining a flashlight into his Jeep. He could dimly make out the dark shape of what appeared to be a rack of lights across the roof of the other vehicle. *Shit! A cop! Damn it!* Stepping behind the rock and sticking his head out, he watched the cop. Maybe he would leave, Morty reflected, but no he was sure to run a check on the vehicle. *Damn!* He went around behind the rock, took off the heavy daypack and climbed to the top to get a better view. As he watched, another police car arrived with its red and blue lights flashing. *Damn! Damn! Damn! Damn!*

What was he to do now? As he sat out of view he saw flashlight beams playing upon the rocks to his right and left for a few moments. There was no time to lose.

As he made his way back to where he'd excavated the gold, Morty tried to formulate a plan of escape. He would have to hike out of there and quickly, but in which direction should he go? To the west was Vasco Road running from the southwest to the northeast until it curved back to the northwest toward Marsh Creek. He thought it best to stay away from the road. He was unfamiliar with the country to the east. To the south was Brushy Peak and he felt certain he could make his way there and then down to Laughlin Road and on to his motel near 580 in Livermore. As he mulled it over, he grew certain that they would surely be patrolling all the roads. He decided to head east. He had some vague recollection of some communities in that direction – maybe he could steal a car. Just then a car alarm's strident warning peal pierced the night from off to the southwest for a few seconds and then was cut off as abruptly as it had begun. It was Morty's car alarm. They were in his car.

Morty was in for a long hike. He needed water and there was no way he could move quickly carrying the heavy gold. He remembered a deep water-filled tinaja he'd once discovered on the top of the rock above a nearby cave. He'd often refilled his water bottle from it in the past. He climbed up there and taking off his pack, he knelt down at the edge. He took out his water bottle and drank the rest of the water in it. Then he dipped it in the tinaja and drank some more. He might not be able to find more water where he was headed, so he thought he'd better make sure he was well hydrated while he had the chance. He filled the water bottle and capped it.

Morty's next move broke his heart, but what good was the gold to him if he got caught? There was no way he could walk fast enough to escape with all that heavy gold in his pack. Opening the large pocket, he shone his flashlight inside. He picked out one of the large octagonal ingots and six of the smaller coins and set them on the ground. Then turning the pack upside down he dumped the rest of the gold into the tinaja. He opened the other two smaller pockets and did the same. He would just have to come back for it at some later time. There was always some impediment to his success, he reflected ruefully. Life was never going to be easy for him. Packing up the seven gold pieces and the water bottle, he made his way down the steep rock face using the familiar foot and handholds he'd ferreted out when he'd first climbed the cliff and discovered the tinaja. He looked around to make sure he wasn't forgetting anything.

After hiking through a rock strewn eastward sloping landscape that he'd never before explored for well over an hour, Morty was exhausted. He took out his water and drank some. He would have to conserve it. He got the bag of trail mix out of his jacket pocket and making a small opening in it, poured some out in his palm, and shoved it in his mouth. He'd have to ration that as well, he figured. There sure wasn't any food to be had out there in the wilderness – none that he knew how to harvest at the start of a rainy California winter. He'd tried to steer a course in a northeasterly direction as best he could with the many large rock outcroppings around which he had to detour. Morty came over a rise and stopped. He surveyed the downward sloping topography descending into the wide San Joaquin Valley. A massive fog bank spread over Clifton Court Forebay and the surrounding valley below. Glancing at his watch he saw it was after three. The moon was now low on the horizon in the west. The temperature was in the low fifties. Morty was cold and exhausted. It was then that he first heard the baying of the hounds.

***

Ian Seare trailed along behind the tracking team. Detective Terrence Teufel, Seare's fellow detective, also came along for the hunt. Shortly after three o'clock they came upon the area where Morty had done his digging. The bloodhounds went back and forth over the ground baying excitedly as they traced Morty's scent from all around the area of the phallic rock formation, to the washout, and over to where Morty had climbed up to the tinaja. The officers found the shovel and the metal detector near the hole where Morty had made his discovery.

Teufel carefully examined the base of the cliff Morty had scaled, but wasn't about to attempt climbing it in the dark. The cliff face was nearly vertical and the prospect of climbing it was treacherous. Teufel abandoned the idea.

He didn't believe Schwartzkopf could have climbed it either. He carefully examined the ground.

Seare contemplated the excavation. Schwartzkopf had been searching for something all right and it looked like he'd found it. He found a large piece of old leather on the ground. He inspected the deep hole under where a large rock had been. Seare bent down and took hold of a ragged piece of leather sticking out of the hole. He gently tugged and shook it until he pulled out what appeared to be part of an old leather saddlebag. Meanwhile, the dogs had picked up Morty's trail and were off again headed east.

***

The sound of the dogs on his trail got Morty moving again. He thought he might be able to maintain the distance between himself and them as long as they didn't loose the hounds. Would they do that? He didn't know. He could only press on as fast as his tired legs would carry him. It was dark now, the moon having disappeared beyond the western horizon some minutes before. Morty had only his flashlight to light the way. The going was rough. On tired legs, sometimes going downhill is as tough as going up. He struggled on for over an hour, forcing himself to keep going, occasionally hearing the hounds baying behind him. Was it his imagination or were they gaining on him?

Finally, Morty had to sit down and rest. Hundred of frogs were taking turns croaking all around him. He drank lustily from his water bottle and ate several handfuls of the trail mix. To hell with rationing it – he needed energy and refreshment now. He heard the hounds. They were getting closer now for sure. As Morty stared back at the misty blackness he thought they might materialize out of it at any moment. His watch read four thirty. He forced himself to his feet and staggered onward.

After having been hounded relentlessly for another forty minutes or so, Morty was delirious. Suddenly he reached the bottom of the hill and came upon level ground. The sky in the east was dawning. He finished the trail mix and drank the last of his water. Morty trudged forward, his legs heavy. At least the walking was much easier on the level ground. He could barely distinguish the outlines of a few large low buildings well off to his left in the foggy morning twilight. After scaling a fence, he found his feet upon a wide concrete paved surface with a bright white line down the middle stretching away in a long straightaway. It was an airfield.

Morty had come upon the lightly used Byron Airport. Walking down the runway, he came to the end. Another runway stretched off at an acute angle to the left, passing in front of the buildings he'd seen. He glanced back the way he'd come, at the buildings, and to the northeast. What were the big, colorful lightbulb shaped things shrouded in fog? He thought he was hallucinating as he staggered forward. Suddenly, as he drew closer, it dawned on him – they were hot air balloons. There must have been twenty-five or thirty of them standing well spaced out in a field across Holey Road, which ran toward the airport. It was a gathering of extreme hot air balloonists preparing to brave the winds of Byron.

The sound of the bloodhounds baying excitedly came to Morty's ears. Turning back he saw them for the first time. They were just emerging from the midst of the morning mist and down onto the level ground of the airfield followed by six or seven men. After momentarily being thwarted by the fence, they got through it. They were running toward him. Morty's hand instinctively felt for his knives on his belt. He drew one out and ran as best he could on his tired legs. He scaled another fence, and made for the field. He struggled to tighten the straps of his pack as he ran. Looking back, he thought they were only about three hundred yards behind now. He crossed the road and ran into the field.

The closest balloon was a checkerboard pattern of bright, multi-colored, diamond-shaped nylon gores. Four men were standing holding ropes attached to the balloon, each about twelve feet away from one of the four corners of the two-man wicker basket. As Morty ran up to the basket he heard one of the men shout, "Hey! Get away from there!"

Morty turned and threw the knife in his hand into a tire of their van. It exploded with a loud pop, the air whooshing out. The vehicle listed toward the left rear wheel. The men momentarily stared at the van with stunned looks on their faces. When they turned back, Morty had already climbed into the gondola. They could see that he had drawn two more knives and had one ready to throw as he screamed hoarsely, "Stay back!"

He swung them around quickly, demonstrating that he was ready to throw at the first man who moved. The police were now only about a hundred yards away and running hard. Morty shouted, "Let go! Let go of the ropes!"

They reluctantly let go and the balloon began to rise. As the police closed to within thirty yards of where the balloon had been, Teufel fired off four shots. Morty ducked down on the far side of the basket. The balloon owner was yelling, "Don't shoot! Don't shoot! You'll blow up my balloon! There's a tank full of propane!" at the officers.

Ian Seare was also remonstrating with Detective Teufel for having fired his weapon. Seare wanted to capture Morty alive, after all he was still only a kid.

Morty was now about a hundred and fifty feet in the air and rising fast. He felt a pain in his left upper arm. A forty caliber round had passed through the kooboo cane basket and grazed him. It was bleeding but not profusely. Morty clapped his right hand over the wound applying pressure. He peeked over the rim of the basket. There was a bustle of activity on the ground. The men who had been holding the ropes and a fifth man piled into another van that had been standing near the balloon and drove rapidly across the field to the road. Morty could see them craning their necks out the windows following the course of the balloon. The dogs were running around in circles where the balloon had been, barking excitedly, their handlers kneeling on the ground attempting to calm them. Seare was barking instructions on his cell phone. Looking over the other side, Morty saw other balloons launching, perhaps to give pursuit in the air. He had escaped but for how long?

Morty sat down and looked at his arm. It was painful and it was still bleeding. He took off his jacket, his sweatshirt, and his T-shirt. It was bitterly cold in the morning air. Getting out his knife, he cut through the collar of his T-shirt and then tore it into long thin strips. He wrapped them around his upper arm as tightly as he could with one hand and tucked the ends in. He put his sweatshirt and jacket back on.

Looking down through the patchy morning mist he judged he must be something like a thousand feet up now. He caught a glimpse of the van tracking his movement from the ground as best it could on a road off to the west. He could hear the sound of traffic on the 205 freeway below. He could catch occasional glimpses of other balloons well below him, but they were all off to the west now. He looked at the apparatus that was emitting a blue flame below the opening of the balloon. Was there a way to crank it up? There was a lever at the bottom and Morty turned it. The flame grew smaller. He turned it the other way, and the flame grew larger. Morty cranked it all the way up. After a short while, the balloon rose more rapidly. Morty sat down to rest and to think.

As far as he could tell there was no way to control the direction of the balloon. He was at the mercy of the winds.

Looking down, he now and then caught sight of the other balloons in the thinning fog below. He'd crossed over the top of them so that they were now far off to the west and fading into the distance fast. His balloon was still rising. Was there a limit to how high he should go? The wind was stronger higher up and it carried him rapidly toward the rising sun. Morty was being carried by a northwesterly wind and after about twenty minutes the balloon had risen to around ten thousand feet. Little did he know that most recreational balloon flights rarely exceed three thousand feet. Morty began to feel woozy. He instinctively knew that it was probably not a good idea to keep going up, so he backed off the lever enough to let the balloon begin descending slowly. He was freezing cold and his arm hurt.

As Morty sat in the gondola of the balloon, he grew despondent. He was tired, hungry, and thirsty. Worst of all, how was it possible to escape pursuit in a giant, brightly colored, slow-moving, uncontrollable contraption? He sat dejectedly for a long time. There was no hope.

Out of nowhere a helicopter buzzed past the balloon. It came around again and hovered a hundred feet from the balloon. One word was emblazoned in large capital letters on the side of the helicopter: POLICE. Morty could see a man sitting to the right of the pilot making a downward motion with his hands. He was telling Morty to land the balloon. It was over.

Looking down at the ground, Morty could see a patchwork quilt of green, gray, and brown rectangles and irregular polygons formed by the agricultural fields of the

Central Valley. In the distance off to his right were the numerous rugged ridges of the Orestimba Wilderness rising thousands of feet above the dividing canyons bottoms below. He passed over the San Joaquin River snaking through the landscape. He thought of jumping out of the balloon, but the thought almost scared him to death. Jumping out of the balloon would be terrifying all the way down until he hit the ground. He was too chicken to do that.

The helicopter was still hovering nearby. Morty reached up and turned the lever on the burner all the way off. The flame went out. At first nothing happened. Then as the air in the envelope began to cool, the balloon began to descend. The descent was gradual at first, but then it began to pick up speed until the balloon was falling at over seven hundred feet a minute. Morty watched transfixed as he rapidly approached the ground. The gondola was headed straight for some high-tension electrical wires. Morty cringed as the balloon careened downward and sideways. He closed his eyes as the basket was about to strike the wires. Nothing happened. Morty looked up and backward. The basket had narrowly cleared the deadly wires.

Looking forward, he saw that he was plunging straight at a two-lane country road. A big red car was coming down the road. The gondola came in fast at an acute angle to the gravel covered asphalt, struck the hard surface and tumbled over, throwing Morty out on the grassy shoulder of the road. The driver slammed on her brakes, bringing the car to a controlled stop but not in time to keep from slamming into the wicker basket and sending it fifteen feet down the road. Morty lay dazed and confused in the grass at the side of the road.

A gray-haired old lady came up to him and asked if he was all right. She said she hadn't seen the balloon until the last second. Morty got up on his hands and knees. The lady told him to lie down; that she'd call an ambulance. He was dimly aware of the sound of a helicopter landing nearby.

That roused Morty. He got up and brushed past the old lady saying, "Sorry, ma'am, I need to borrow your car," and got into her car.

He heard the lady say, "Not my Cadillac!" He saw men running from the helicopter, which had landed in a field adjacent to the road. He put the car into reverse turning the steering wheel to the left, then when the car was perpendicular to the road, he put it in drive and swung the steering wheel to the right. He hit the gas and the big Caddy accelerated smoothly, though not without a lot of yaw as he made the turn and straightened out. In the rearview mirror, he saw the men stop running momentarily and then, turning around, they ran back toward the helicopter, leaving Detective Terrence Teufel at the scene to attend to the old woman and the balloon. Morty had lost his pack in the crash. He wondered where he was.

Morty knew he had to think fast for the helicopter would be in the air and on his tail shortly. Was there a turn off close by where he could find some cover from the eyes in the sky among trees? Could there be a tunnel nearby through which he could make his escape? Should he ditch the car and set out on foot? The road was lined with flat agricultural fields on both sides as far as he could see, offering absolutely no place to hide. Morty slowed to negotiate a series of bends after which the road stretched out for miles as straight and flat as the airport runway he'd walked along that morning.

The helicopter was on him now, apparently trying to intimidate him by flying low and close behind the car when it could. Morty accelerated to eighty miles an hour, flying past the fields and the occasional farmhouses. He had never driven even close to that fast before. Suddenly an intersection came into view. He roared over the words 'STOP' and 'AHEAD' painted on the roadway, barely registering their import, before he reached the intersection.

As he steeled himself to shoot right on through, a blue car pulled into the intersection from the right. Morty jerked the steering wheel to the left and jammed on the brakes, swerved in front of the car and went skidding into an almond orchard at fifty miles an hour, snapping off one tree before coming to an abrupt halt against the trunk of another.

III

Morty had crashed in Ceres. The ambulance had taken him to Memorial Hospital in Modesto. When he awoke, he was handcuffed to the bed and a police officer was posted outside the door. His father was seated at his bedside. When he saw that Morty had opened his eyes, he held his hand. After a while, Morty said, "I had it, Dad. I had the gold."

His father replied soothingly, "Just lay back and rest, Morty. You've been through quite an ordeal from what I hear." Morty just closed his eyes and shook his head in answer.

Later, the doctor told Morty he was lucky he'd been driving a late model car. The '97 Cadillac's airbags had saved his life. He hadn't been wearing a seatbelt. He had suffered a mild concussion. His nose and the ulna of his left forearm were broken. He had abrasions all over his body and his hearing was impaired. The doctor had treated and sewn up the bullet wound on his left upper arm. He said Morty should make a full recovery.

The following day, Morty was arraigned at the Stanislaus County Superior Court. His father had hired him an attorney. Morty was charged with involuntary manslaughter in the death of Clarissa Phalen, his mother, in December of 1994 when he was a minor; forgery for the Washington driver's license, two counts of license plate theft, aggravated assault in the case of Fritz Utrecht, trespassing on restricted park lands; resisting arrest, two counts of grand theft – the hot air balloon and 1997 Cadillac DeVille – and reckless driving. Morty pled not guilty. The judge considered Morty a flight risk and denied bail. Morty was remanded to the custody of the Stanislaus County Sheriff, to be detained at the Stanislaus County Jail in Modesto, initially in the medical ward.

Ian Seare and his fellow detectives conducted a thorough search of the balloon, the area where it came down, and the car. Morty's backpack containing an empty stainless steel water bottle and an empty trail mix and beef jerky bags had been recovered. Curiously enough, there was no mention of the seven gold pieces that had been in Morty's backpack in the police report.

After two weeks in the medical ward of the Stanislaus County Jail, Morty was transferred to a dual occupancy cell. His fellow inmate was a strongly built, middle aged guy, with a rugged weather beaten face, hooked nose, blue eyes, a space between his two front teeth and a receding hairline which his prison haircut did nothing to hide. He watched as the guard put Morty in the cell.

Morty lay down on his bunk and turned his thoughts elsewhere. How long would he be in jail? He didn't think they had any solid evidence against him for the more serious crimes of which he was accused. Despite his predicament, Morty was still obsessed with the problem of how was he going to get the gold he'd dumped in the tinaja once he got out of jail. He tried to imagine different scenarios whereby he could get to the tinaja, get the gold out of it, and safely get away. Maybe he could parachute in, get the gold, and fly out of there in a jetpack like he'd once seen in a Bond movie. Morty briefly recollected the night he'd seen the film at the Oaks Theatre in Berkeley. What was the title? *Thunderball*. However he ultimately went after the gold, it had better be soon, for the tinaja would dry up in the long hot summer months and the gold would be lying there exposed. For once Morty was glad the park district was restricting access to the caves. Still, there were undoubtedly other rogue hikers like Morty who'd be clandestinely hiking out there.

Morty would have to be much smarter than he had been in his last attempt. He was still berating himself severely for the stupid mistakes he'd made. Why hadn't he taken the necessary precautions? He seemed to always assume that things would work out in his favor. Why did he continue to do that when things never did seem to go his way? It was just his nature, he guessed, but this next time would have to be different. Once again he began to dream about the material goods he'd buy with the money he'd get from selling all the gold. The house he'd have specially designed for himself and fill with the finest furnishings, the thirty seat movie theater, the multi-car garage filled with exotic automobiles, the Olympic sized swimming pool… Perhaps he'd buy a yacht… The list went on and on. It was plain that gold fever still coursed virulently through Morty's veins.

"What're ya in for, kid?" The question startled Morty out of his reverie.

"Well, I'm charged with a number of crimes, but they won't be able to make the big one stick, I don't think."

"Big one?"

"Involuntary manslaughter."

"Really? Ya don't look like yuv got it in ya, kid. Tell me about it."

"It's a long story."

"Kid, we've got nuttin but time in here. What's yer name anyway?"

"Morty Schwartzkopf. What's yours?"

"Walter Higginson, call me Walt."

Morty told Walt what had happened to him over the last few years from the time of his discovery in the hills, his fight with his mother and her death, to his waking up in the hospital in Modesto. He left out critical details that he either didn't want to share or which would have revealed too much about where the gold was hidden. When he was finished, Walt said, "Wow, kid, that's some tale. So, I suppose when ya get outta here yer plannin' on makin' another play for that gold."

"You bet. Wouldn't you? I was just considering the possibilities."

"Supposin' ya do get all that gold. What're ya plannin' on doin' with it?"

Morty told Walt about all the things he planned to purchase, from a big house to fancy cars. Walt just shook his head and said disgustedly, "Damn, Morty, for a while thar I thought ya might be some kinda revolutionary. I had hopes, but now I see yer just as nefarious as all the rest."

"Nefar… what? Who?"

"All the corrupt, wealthy pig shots in the world, Morty. All the money-grubbing, power hungry assholes who exploit hard working men and women, keepin' them down, and plunder the world's resources just to aggrandize their own massive egos and amass astronomical riches. I mean, how much money does one person need in this world, Morty? Is it right that a billionaire jet set comprised of a small fraction of individuals lives out their rapacious, gluttonous existence in opulence while the masses struggle to make ends meet, many of them livin' on the streets, or even starvin' to death?"

Morty guessed he'd struck a nerve. "So… what are you saying?"

"I'm sayin' yer no better than they are. Ya know the trouble with you, Morty? I seen it right off. I'll tell ya what the trouble with you is: ya don't stand for nothin'. Ya don't care about nothing, Morty. Yer the classic rebel without a cause. Did ya ever see that film? I guess not. James Dean. Yuv got no ambition, Morty. Ya rebel against the forces in the world that are keeping ya down, but then as soon as ya get yers, ya become one of 'em. Pitiful."

Morty didn't have any answer to Walt's harangue. He was stinging and stewing over the harshly worded criticism of his dreams. At first, he just clammed up, feeling hurt and disinterested in continuing the conversation. He lay down again, sulking. Who was this guy to disparage his dreams like that? After a while, he calmed down a bit and reflecting on what Walt had said, he realized he was right. He didn't stand for anything. He was after the gold for himself, to enrich himself – it was true. Wasn't that the American dream? Walt was right. His dreams were hollow and selfish. What had he planned to do if he got rich? Enjoy life. Have fun. Party all the time. Had he any plans to do good? To somehow make the world a better place? To help anyone out? Did he have any ambition to go to school or forge a career? No. He lay on his bunk for hours turning such thoughts over in his mind. What did he plan to do with his life? What did he care about?

The next day, Morty thought he'd find out a bit more about his self-styled rebel of a cellmate. "So, Walt, what are *you* in for?"

"What am I in for? Me and a couple of anarchist acquaintances of mine busted into the animal research lab of a local university and freed all of their guinea pigs, rats, and frogs. Animal testing is a travesty. Vivisection is inhumane and should not be tolerated under any circumstances. Almost got away, but I got nabbed 'cause some misguided soul had spotted my van parked on a nearby street and gotten my license plate number. Gave it to the cops when she heard about the break-in."

"So rescuing lab animals is your cause?"

"You could say that. It wasn't the first time I was involved in something like that. We once freed over a thousand minks from a fur farm in Oregon. Ya might not agree with what we did, but I'm tellin' ya that human beings should not be slaughterin' innocent little animals so they can strut about in their furs showin' off how stylish they are. Reprehensible! In this day and age we have the technology to make coats that are plenty warm out of plant fibers or even petroleum – but that's another issue you'd better not get me started on.

"Did a little stint with Oceanpeace too tryin' to prevent them Japanese from killin' whales down under. That was some dangerous shit, I'm tellin' ya. Our boat got rammed more 'n a few times when we blocked their whalin' ship's path. But we hindered 'em 'n' kept 'em from killin' some of them whales. Magnificent creatures those. No excuse in hell to be slaugterin' 'em.

"I once did six months fer scalin' the Golden Gate Bridge to hang a banner protestin' the loggin' of the ancient redwoods in Humboldt County. Snarled up traffic fer five hours. Had to raise them Marin County bastards' awareness, ya know. What's the loss of five hours of their time compared to the loss of those fifteen hundred year old trees? The police didn't take too kindly to me and my friends' refusal to obey their commands, but it was worth it. Have ya been to see the Redwoods, Morty? I just love them trees! Did you know that a few of those ancient redwoods have been around since the times of

Muhammad! Jesus! Moses! of… of… Buddha! Bodhidharma! And… and… Lao Zi!

"Ya know? It's a crime to cut them trees down!

"Ya see, Morty, most folks are just like you. Complacent. Complacent and ignorant. They don't know the truth about what's going on and they probably prefer it that way. They go blithely on with their daily lives and as long as they get theirs, they don't care where it comes from or how it comes. If they knew the truth they'd have a hard time justifying their lifestyle, so they just don't go there."

Morty could think of no appropriate response to this monologue. He had obviously struck another one of Walt's nerves. Who was this guy? Finally he asked, "What do you do for money while you're running around the world crusading?"

"Oh, I do a little acting now and then. Maybe you've seen reruns of the sitcom I once did called *Bottoms Up!*… No, I guess not. I played a lovelorn bartender. I've acted in a few films, as well. Ever seen *White Men Can Sky*? No? What about *Cash Caravan*? No? OK, OK, those may have been some of my lesser known films. But surely you've heard of *Indelicate Proposition*. No? What are you, Morty – some kinda troglodyte? Ya don't get out much, do ya?"

After a pause, Morty asked, "What do you miss most from the outside?"

Without hesitation Walt replied, "Mort – may I call you Mort?" Getting a nod from Morty, he went on, "Mort, first thing I get out of here, I'm headin' to my favorite restaurant, Café Grateful, over in Berkeley. I'm cravin' their macro bowl and nori rolls... cashew lemon cheesecake – everything really. I love everything on their menu. I go there first thing whenever I'm in the Bay Area. See, I'm a raw food vegan, Mort."

Morty queried, "Raw food? You mean you don't eat cooked food?"

"That's right. The food in here's killin' me, slow poisonin', man."

"So you only eat... salad?"

"No, no – there're all kinds of dishes you can make from nuts and veggies, mushrooms, fruits... you'd be surprised at all the stuff they make. So fresh and good for the body too. You should give it a try; it's ultra healthy."

"Why no cooking though?"

"'Cause cookin' destroys the enzymes and vitamins in the food, man."

Morty didn't know too much about enzymes and the raw food movement, but he could see that Walt was a zealot.

When Morty wasn't shooting the breeze with Walt Higginson, he spent most of his time reading. He especially liked reading what he thought of as classic literature, and the prison library had a tolerably decent collection. Morty enjoyed reading Dickens and Doyle, Twain and Poe, Hugo and Dumas, Nietzsche and Kafka, Dostoyevsky and Tolstoy.

Once when Morty had his nose buried in a book, Walt said, "I see you really enjoy reading, Morty. Mostly fiction. I'm wondering if you would find this little book interesting." He held up a slim volume. "Have you ever read the *Dao De Jing*?" Morty shook his head. "It's not a novel. It's an ancient Chinese philosophical text. I've spent many hours pondering the wisdom expressed in its pages. This particular volume is the Wu Ming translation which of all the many translations that have been made over the last century plus is my absolute favorite. The translator really understood the essence of the Daoist philosophy expressed in its eighty-one brief chapters. Nothing is known about him, or her as the case may be, except that he or she translated the classical Chinese into English. The translator used the pseudonym 'Wu Ming' which, without the benefit of the Chinese characters, has an ambiguous meaning. It could mean 'Without Name' as in anonymous, or it could mean 'Without Understanding' as in I am only an ignorant translator. Either way it adheres to the book's philosophy of modesty and self-effacement. It is also a simple volume without all the frills and glossy graphics of most recent publications, which detract from the simplicity of the message. It's just plain paper hand-bound in the classic Chinese style with exposed stitching. You won't find it in any bookstore. It's not for sale. The translator was not looking to profit from his or her interpretation of the classical Chinese, only to bring the ancient wisdom to English readers. It was given to me by a friend who had been given it by a friend and now I'm giving it to you." Walt handed the slim well-read volume to Morty.

"Gee, thanks, Walt. What a special gift – I'll treasure reading it, I'm sure." Morty examined the well-thumbed book. It had held up well. It was curiously bound – unlike any other book he'd ever seen. It appeared to have been printed on sheets of standard 8.5 by 11 inch letter paper, however each sheet had been carefully folded in half so that the actual pages were 8.5 inches tall and 5.5 inches wide. The open ends of the folded sheets were bound by some kind of rather thick waxen thread, probably linen, so that the folds formed the outer edges of the pages. Thus each page was double thick and had empty space on the inside of the folds. The book had been bound by poking or drilling eight evenly spaced holes about half an inch in from the open edges of the folded pages. Then the waxen thread had been run up and down from hole to hole on both the front and the back and around the spine of the book to each hole as well as the top and bottom edges of the two holes at the ends. Morty observed a small knot where the ends of the thread had been tied off directly over the bottom hole on the back of the book. It was a nifty hand-binding technique.

Morty looked at the cover. The title was in small print in the middle about a third of the way down from the top and said simply, *Dao De Jing*. Centered just below it was 'Lao Zi'. Near the bottom it said 'Translated by Wu Ming'.

Morty looked at Walt and asked, "Lao Zi?"

"The purported Chinese author's name."

"Purported?"

"The *Dao De Jing* is over twenty-five hundred years old. Its authorship is shrouded in mystery and legend."

"Twenty-five hundred years – wow! It was written well before the common era. Chinese sure is an old language. I once read that English only developed as a language in the fifth century of the common era and modern English didn't develop until something like the thirteenth century."

"Chinese is the world's oldest continuously used language. The *Dao De Jing* was written in classical Chinese however, which would not necessarily be easy for your average Chinese person to read and fully comprehend without special study. Nevertheless, since Chinese isn't an alphabetic script, many of the characters haven't changed in form over the years. There are some obscure characters, but with a bit of study one can learn to read the ancient Chinese classics which were written centuries before the time of Christ."

"You seem to know a lot about the Chinese language."

"Yes, I lived in Taiwan for three years after I finished college and learned to speak Mandarin and read and write Chinese passably while there. I was particularly interested in learning to read the ancient Chinese texts, so I studied classical Chinese as well. I've been working on improving my Chinese ever since."

Morty opened the book and leafed through it. Each of the eighty-one so-called 'chapters' consisted of only a few sentences or phrases, as it were, as there was a notable lack of punctuation. The longest book Morty had ever read, of which he was justly proud, was an English translation of Victor Hugo's *Les Miserables*, which was over a thousand pages long. Morty could tell at a glance that the *Dao De Jing* would easily be the shortest book he'd ever read as an adult.

"This is really cool – thanks again, Walt."

"You're welcome. I look forward to discussing the ideas expressed in there with you once you've had a chance to read it. Chapter eighty-one, the last chapter, sums up some of the ideas I want you to consider. Here let me see that for a moment. It says, 'Sages don't accumulate possessions, since acting on people's behalf is more than its own reward, since in helping people, they themselves have a surplus. Heaven's way is beneficial and not harmful. The sage's Dao serves and doesn't contend.'" He handed the book back to Morty.

Morty turned to the last chapter and read it again, then sat engrossed in thought. Then he turned to the beginning and began to read.

One day, Walt asked again about the manslaughter with which Morty was charged. Morty hesitated. A sea of emotions came roiling to the surface, and Morty's eyes welled up. Suddenly he blurted out, "It was an accident. I never meant to kill her. I caught her in my room taking my money and gold. As I wrested them from her hands she fell back and hit her head on the corner of my terrarium. I knew she was dead just looking at her. I should have called nine one one, but I was afraid. So I ransacked the whole house to make it look like some thieves had been searching for something, and I told the cops that the coins I'd found and my money had been stolen. They're on to me, but I don't think they can prove anything."

Walt only suggested, "Maybe you should come clean, Mort. After all, it was an accident. Just something to think about."

Over the course of the couple of months that they were incarcerated together, Morty learned a lot from Walt about subjects he'd never even heard of before. The more he talked to Walt, the more Morty was impressed by his commitment to the causes he believed in and his willingness to put his skin on the line to make a difference. Morty spent a lot of time reflecting on his own life and thinking about what Walt had said about his lack of ambition and ambivalence about the many injustices in the world.

***

At the preliminary hearing, the judge ruled that the evidence against Ari Grunbergin the involuntary manslaughter of Clarissa Phalen case was insufficient for Morty to be tried on that charge and that the evidence against him in the aggravated assault of Fritz Utrecht was purely circumstantial. Both charges were dismissed. He was held over to be tried on the other charges.

At his felony arraignment, the judge determined that the prosecution had presented sufficient evidence to hold Morty over for trial. At the second pretrial conference,

Morty's attorney negotiated a plea deal to settle his case. On the advice of his attorney, Morty accepted the plea bargain. In light of the fact that he had no previous record, Morty was to pay fines totaling thirty-five hundred dollars and be released for time served. He had been in jail for two and a half months. He would be on probation for two years.

While he was in jail, Morty had decided that when he was released he would stay in the Bay Area. When he finally did get out, he rented an apartment on Hopyard in Pleasanton. He went to the DMV, registered his Jeep, and got a legitimate California driver's license and legitimate license plates. He got insurance.

Morty checked his backpack when it was returned to him by the police. There was no gold in it, of course. Morty had expected that, but he didn't dare complain. Far more gold was awaiting his return to the tinaja and the worst thing he could do would be to attract attention to the fact that he'd discovered a hoard of Gold Rush era gold coins. Morty suddenly realized that the spare smart key to his Jeep was missing. He was sure he had put it in the small pocket of his backpack. He did want to complain about that, but in the end decided it was a lost cause, like the seven gold pieces he'd never see again. "Damn police!" Morty swore. Those coins had to be worth half a million dollars, at least.

Detective Teufel shadowed Morty when he wasn't busy with police business. Instinctively, he knew that Morty had something to hide. He had a hunch that Morty would visit the spot at the Vasco Caves again, and when

Morty did, Teufel wanted to intercept him on his return journey.

Morty's conversations with Walt Higginson in jail had profoundly affected his Weltanschauung. He was still obsessed with obtaining the gold he'd hidden, but his ideas of how he would use it if he could get it had changed. Morty knew deep down that Walt was right when he said that Morty was self-centered and that his dreams of how he'd spend his wealth had been hedonistic and myopic. He did want to make something of his life. He did want a cause he could believe in – one to which he could dedicate himself. But what cause? Morty needed some time to think, but at the same time he needed a distraction to relax his mind. He decided to do something he'd wanted to do for many years but had never had the chance to do before. He decided to visit the Monterey Bay Aquarium.

Ever since Morty had been a kid he'd wanted to go to the Monterey Bay Aquarium. His mom just never seemed to be able to make time or have the desire to take him there. Now that he could drive and had his Cherokee back, there was nothing to stop him from going. Morty had read in an article about the aquarium that you could take a behind the scenes tour to see how they run the place. He called ahead to reserve a spot on the tour and then drove down to Monterey three days later on a Tuesday.

Morty was blown away by the size and scope of the exhibits at the Monterey Bay Aquarium. They had three gigantic aquariums housing a splendid collection of local and not so local fish species. Numerous smaller tanks and miniature habitats were filled with the amazing diversity of organisms that live in the environs of the Monterey Bay kelp forest, tidepools, estuaries, mangrove swamps, the pelagic zone, and coral reefs. From sea jellies to leafy sea dragons, sea turtles to hammerhead sharks, puffins to plovers, sea otters to tuna, giant octopi to ancient nautili, and everything in between, around every corner was another example of the fabulous diversity of the fascinating creatures that live in the ocean environment. The successful installation and maintenance of the three-story giant kelp aquarium, including pumping in natural seawater form the bay, was a Herculean achievement in and of itself.

Equally as impressive as the spectacular exhibits was the Monterey Bay Aquarium's commitment to preservation of ocean ecosystems through research, rescue, and education programs. The aquarium's work with orphaned and stranded sea otter pups is continually pioneering new methods for rescuing, caring for, and releasing these adorable marine mammals. Surgically implanted radio transmitters help aquarium biologists track sea otters that have been released to determine whether or not they are successfully adapting to living in the wild once again. Released otters have given birth to pups in the wild – the surest indication of the ultimate success of the aquarium's efforts. The aquarium also coordinates with other marine institutions to research, track, and help conserve threatened sea turtles, tuna, and sharks.

Morty came away from his day at the aquarium in awe of what the foresight, vision, and determination of a few dedicated individuals had been able to accomplish. Once, in that place, sardines were netted by the thousands, dumped in redwood hoppers just off the coast, sucked into the cannery through huge pipes, gutted by the millions, packed in cans like… well, sardines… cooked, sauced, sealed, and cooked again. Today, on the very spot, sardines are exalted as a critical part of the marine food chain, valued as a harbinger of the state of the ocean ecosystem, and exhibited to the public in shimmering silver schools. A place that had once been set up to exploit the abundant and seemingly inexhaustible resources of the sea had been transformed into a shining beacon of stewardship and knowledge of the incredibly diverse yet threatened ocean environments which cover three quarters of the Earth.

His trip to the aquarium motivated Morty to start building a menagerie of his own again. He wanted to have an aquarium and a couple of terrariums in his apartment like the ones he'd had in his mother's house, only better. He knew he should start small. He drove over to the East Shore Vivarium in Berkeley to see their collection of critters for sale and get some idea of what he might like to keep. He was most interested in keeping native California species since he planned to capture the animals himself rather than buy them from a vivarium. The one thing Morty loved to do in life more than anything else was to go on his hiking excursions and catch animals that he could raise and study at home.

While at the East Shore Vivarium, Morty saw many fascinating reptiles, amphibians, arachnids, and arthropods, but the one that piqued his interest the most was the California mountain kingsnake. The specimen they had was about three feet long and with its red, white, and black rings it was the most beautiful snake Morty had ever seen. Morty learned as much as he could about creating a suitable environment for a California mountain kingsnake from the herpetologists at the East Shore Vivarium. Later he did some online research to determine its range, habits, and how to capture one. One day in mid June, Morty drove up to the mountains to go herping. Late in the evening, he returned with a fetid bundle tied up in a pillowcase.

A couple of weeks after Morty had returned from his inspirational trip to the Monterey Bay Aquarium, he drove over to Byron Airport to check out the scene of his narrow and hairy, albeit temporary, escape. He examined the airport grounds, and the surrounding property stretching off west to the foothills of the Diablo Range. While examining maps of the area, he'd noticed a place north of the Byron Airport called the Old Byron Hot Springs Hotel. In researching the property, Morty had learned that it had once been a world-renowned resort in the late nineteenth and early twentieth centuries but had fallen on hard times after the Great Depression. During World War Two, the U.S Army had taken over the struggling resort and turned it into a secret interrogation center for Japanese and German prisoners of war. They had called it Camp Tracy.

Shortly after the war, in 1946, the property was acquired by the Greek Orthodox Church, and they used it as a spiritual retreat and mission. They christened it Mission St. Paul. After a decade, the property was sold again and then proceeded to change hands numerous times in the intervening years while falling further and further into a state of disrepair.

Morty decided to make his second attempt at retrieving the gold by hiking into the Vasco Caves from the old hot springs resort to the northeast. A private road ran east into the abandoned property from Byron Hot Springs Road. From the back of the property, Morty figured he could strike out in a southwesterly direction across the fields and over the rolling hills to the area of the Vasco Caves. He calculated he would need to camp out for two nights to accomplish his objective. He went to RAI in Berkeley and bought himself a green backpack, T-shirts, pants and a Sombriolet sun hat that would blend in with the verdant grasses of the spring landscape in Contra Costa County. He also purchased a light sleeping bag and a small tent. For food Morty figured he could subsist on trail mix and beef jerky for a couple of days. He filled two liter, stainless-steel water bottles. He would have to find water along the way. Surely the tinaja would still be full, wouldn't it?

On the first of April, Morty took BART from Pleasanton to Nineteenth Street in downtown Oakland and then transferred to a Pittsburg/Bay Point train. From the BART Station, he hopped a bus to Brentwood. He ate a good dinner at a Greek restaurant and then called for a taxi to take him out to the town of Byron twelve miles away. The taxi driver dropped him off at the Byron Inn near the corner of the Byron Highway and Byron Hot Springs Road. A few minutes' walk down the Byron Hot Springs Road brought him to the entry road to the Old Byron Hot Springs Resort on the right.

Teufel had been following Morty at the start of his excursion, but he had anticipated being able to follow Morty by car, and he was caught off guard when Morty parked at the Pleasanton BART Station and walked in toting his backpack. Though Morty hadn't the slightest idea that he was being tailed, he lost Teufel easily anyway on public transportation.

Morty leapt over the metal barrier gate into the grounds. He walked briskly down the entry road to get away from the public road as quickly as possible. He was now trespassing on private property and needed to traverse it as quickly as possible. Morty walked down the ornamental pepper tree lined private road for about seven tenths of a mile until he came to the abandoned hotel. The area in front and to the south of the old hotel was planted with numerous palm trees. The founding father of the resort, Louis Risdon Mead, had filled in the salt basin in front of the first hotel with twelve feet of good soil and created an oasis in the midst of an alkali plain. Besides the palms, there had been scattered evergreens, oleander trees, and a multitude of flowers. Now it was more of a desert, only the hardiest of the plants having survived the years of neglect, chief among them the palms.

Built from 1912 to 1914, the four-story brick and concrete third hotel building was one of architect James W. Reid's less inspired creations. In character, it paled in comparison to the previous hotel, also designed by Reid. The second hotel had been inspired by Spanish and Moorish architecture and had been an immediate sensation, which drew people from all over to the springs. The three-story frame stucco structure's signature elements were its distinctive twin turrets and broad veranda. Reid had also been the architect of the historic Hotel del Coronado near San Diego, and later designed the Cliff House and the Fairmont Hotel in San Francisco and numerous luxurious cinemas in the Bay Area including the Grand Lake in Oakland and the Sebastiani Theatre in Sonoma. Sadly, the second and most charming of the Byron Hot Springs hotels burned to the ground in 1912 after only a decade in operation. The first hotel on the property, which opened in 1878 and had been built by remodeling and connecting smaller buildings on the property, had also burned down in 1901. Therefore, the overriding concern in the construction of the third hotel seemed to have been to make it fireproof rather than ornate. In this regard Reid was successful, as the third hotel, of brick and concrete construction, was still standing eighty-four years later.

In addition to striving to make the third hotel fireproof, numerous improvements were made to supply fire protection. Two miles of pipes were laid to a pumping station on the San Joaquin River. Water was pumped from there to three water tanks that held a quarter of a million gallons on a nearby hill to the north. The water was released from the reservoirs to fire hydrants installed around the structures on the property, which included numerous small cottages. It was an impressive effort, but it was like locking the stable door after your prize horse has been stolen.

The once glorious resort hotel was now but a forlorn and abandoned carapace of its former self. It had been beset by unscrupulous vandals and taggers, who had stolen design elements and defaced the walls with their self-indulgent graffiti. The taggers had selfishly and disgustingly despoiled the appearance of the historically significant building, inside and out. In their perverse desire to tag wherever they go, they leave a visual marker analogous to and no better than a dog marking its territory with the scent of its urine. Morty had never understood the desire to carry cans of spray paint around in order to do that. Oh, the uneducated.

As he walked past the southern end, the former hotel building stretched off to the north for some fifty yards. Its numerous sashless windows and doorless doorways were regularly spaced rectangular black holes in its façade. The almost complete absence of architectural flourishes made it look more like the remnant of a college dormitory than an upscale hotel. The debris strewn remains of a stairway into the hotel jutted out toward where Morty stood near one end.

He had read about people who had entered the deserted hotel and the stories they told about strange noises they'd heard and ghosts they'd supposedly seen. He wondered how many people had died there in the eighty-four years of the building's existence. Hotel guests? Japanese or German prisoners of war? Members of the Greek Orthodox Church? Vagrants? Could the property itself be haunted? Morty knew that the victims of the Great Byron Train Wreck of 1902 had been brought to the springs when the second hotel was standing. They had included an entire Chinese wedding party, all of whom perished in the disaster. Early California explorers and settlers in the eighteenth and nineteenth centuries had visited the springs. The springs had been used for centuries by American Natives and are considered by them to be hallowed ground. All these thoughts of ghosts and the faded history of the place while standing near the creepy shell of the hotel in the fading twilight, sent a chill down Morty's spine and, telling himself that he didn't believe in ghosts, he moved quickly onward toward the rear of the property.

Who would now guess that this abandoned oasis at the foot of the Diablo Range had once been the playground of famous writers, socialites, Hollywood movie stars, and professional athletes, like the San Francisco Seals? They played golf, tennis, croquet, and held spring training. They rode horses. They ate fine cuisine. They drank Joseph

Kennedy whiskey during prohibition. They swam in a bubbling wooden swimming pool and soaked in marble-lined bathhouses. *Laissez les bons temps rouler* – until the Great Depression hit and the good times were over.

Who would now guess that the U.S. Army and Navy had jointly purchased the resort during World War Two, in 1942, and turned the hotel into such an ultra top secret interrogation center that no one would know what had gone on there until over forty-seven years after the war had ended, in 1992? That during the two and a half years of the camp's operation, they interrogated over thirty-five hundred Japanese prisoners of war there in the Old Byron Springs Hotel? Little evidence remains that a Joint Interrogation Center (JIC) once existed in the old hotel. They had converted the fourth floor to twenty-two two-man cells with false ceilings, vents between bathrooms to encourage communication, and listening devices. Caucasian interrogators, trained in Japanese language and culture, had been paired with Nisei Japanese American interrogators, and had extracted valuable intelligence in the four bugged interrogation rooms on the third floor without resorting to torture.

The interrogators' quarters had been on the third floor and the second floor, on the latter of which the kitchen and dining areas were also located. The first floor was devoted to the POW in-processing station, administrative offices, two recording equipment control rooms and four soundproof listening rooms. There's no sign of the rectangular perimeter fence that had been erected around the building or the four guard towers, one at each corner. There's precious little proof of Army Camp Tracy that had surrounded the JIC. Photographs of the facility had been prohibited.

Who would now guess that the Papago Park Seven had been sent to Camp Tracy in '44? The captured German U-boat sailors were alleged to have hung a shipmate, whom they believed to be a traitor, in one of the shower rooms at the POW camp located in Papago Park, Arizona. Interrogations and bugged private conversations at Camp Tracy led to their conviction for murder. Even though World War Two had already ended, a mass execution of the seven men was carried out at Fort Leavenworth, Kansas in the fall of '45. They were strung up in an abandoned elevator shaft. Some maintained the army was taking revenge for having been humiliated by an escape attempt by a number of German prisoners of war incarcerated at the Papago Park POW Camp on the Winter Solstice of the previous year.

Who would now guess that Primate Athemagoras had acquired ownership from Mae Mead Reid in 1946? She had been Louis Risdon Mead's wife for eleven years until he died in 1918 and had subsequently married the architect, James W. Reid, who died in 1944. Ms. Reid bequeathed the property to the Greek Orthodox Church. The bishop had a vision of turning the property into the center of church activities in its western diocese, which encompassed ten western states and part of Canada. On December 8th, 1948, the now Grand Patriarch

Athemagoras presided over a ceremony to consecrate the then former Byron Hot Springs as Mission St. Paul and Reverend Pappagiannacopoulos as Abbott. The retreat lasted a decade.

Who would now guess that Byron boys had attended summer camp at the mission from 1948 to 1956 and slept out under the stars in army platform tents, swum in the wooden pool, and drunk from the springs?

A waxing gibbous moon had just risen above the horizon in the east. The moon cast an eerie glow on the dewy landscape. Morty had brought along a pair of thick gloves to deal with scaling fences. He encountered a few before he reached the hills. He pitched his tent and got some shuteye.

In the early morning, he hiked up a nascent ravine. He climbed a hill to see the stand of trees growing on top. They were Palmer oaks, no more than ten feet tall. A southern species, it was unusual to find a stand growing so far north. In some Palmer stands, all of the trees have been found to be genetically identical, making the whole stand, in essence, one tree. At thirteen thousand years of age, Palmer oak clones are one of the oldest living plants. A relic from the Pleistocene that ended up in northern California through a bit of plate tectonic legerdemain. Morty examined the small spiny leathery leaves, hairy-capped acorns, and bark of the Palmers.

A barely discernible path led around the perimeter of the grove. Morty went anticlockwise. Morty paused to examine some rather large scat. A score more paces down the path brought him up short. The remains of a partially eaten deer lay stinking just off the path. Morty held his breath as he rushed past. Suddenly it dawned on Morty that the scat and the dead deer could mean the presence of only one thing – a mountain lion. He glanced at his paltry duo of throwing knives in their sheath on his belt. Would he have the nerve to stand his ground and throw his knives at a big cat? Would they even faze a panther? Why hadn't he taken the time to replace the knife he'd thrown into the tire of the hot air balloonists' van? Morty stood petrified, staring at the deep shadows under the diminutive Palmer oaks. He imagined he heard a low growling sound. That got Morty moving swiftly on his way.

All of a sudden, there it was, stalking him in the shadows of the oaks. A huge cougar. A low, terrifying growl emanated from the big cat periodically. It watched Morty through the trees and paralleled him leisurely as he hurried along the path trying to act like he wasn't hurrying along the path. Morty knew that running would be the worst thing to do. That would surely trigger the chase instinct in the big cat and it would swiftly overtake him. He needed to edge away slowly without giving any appearance of trying to flee. This also meant facing the beast.

Morty steeled his nerves and adopted an air of bravado, staring at the puma. That also appeared to be the wrong thing to do, because it made the cat let out a fierce snarl. Morty decided not to make any more eye contact. He sidled along the path in a state of panic until he came to a huge rock outcropping that cut horizontally across the slope. Once behind the rock and out of sight of the ferocious feline, he ran for his life down the hill and onto a trail along the watercourse in the ravine at its base and up the next rise before he stopped for a breather. There was no sign of the cat. Whew! It must not have been hungry.

As Morty came over the next rise slaloming through the wind turbines, he recognized the territory he'd traversed on his flight from the police dog team. He knew exactly where he was. He trekked back along the route, eager to distance himself from the area of the Catamount and the incessant whopping of the damn glorified windmills. He crossed the clearing, passed the phallic rock, the cave in which he'd found shelter from the deluge, and the spot of his discovery. He noted that the shovel and metal detector he'd left there were gone. It was a good thing that he'd wiped them down, he thought.

He went on down the slope to the huge rock on top of which was the tinaja. Morty paused for a few minutes to catch his breath, then he climbed up to the tinaja with difficulty. He sat down near the edge. He heard a couple of plop plop sounds and knew the pool was inhabited by at least two frogs. He took off his backpack, his sneakers, his socks. He rolled up his jeans and swung his feet into the water. The cool water felt good on his sore feet. He scooched forward until his knees were in the water too. His pants legs got wet, so he got up and took them off.

The pool was teeming with fairy shrimp. As Morty sat there tranquilly, the two frogs surfaced. California red-legged frogs. This now federally listed, threatened species of frog was once widespread. The forty-niner goldminers would often eat them. Mark Twain's celebrated jumping frog of Calaveras County was a California red-legged frog. When their numbers declined, humans, in their infinite wisdom, brought in bullfrogs from back east to supply the demand. The larger bullfrogs pushed the red-legged frogs to the brink of extinction. *It just never seems to work out when human beings meddle with Mother Nature*, Morty reflected.

Morty took out the swim goggles and waterproof flashlight he'd brought. He tested the flashlight. No problem. He took off his T-shirt. The tinaja was about six feet in diameter and circular except for a blip on the far side stretching out to the precipice. Morty put on his goggles and slid on his bottom until he was completely in the water. The displaced water surged over the blip and on down the cliff face, cascading down to the ground twenty-five feet below.

At first, Morty hunched up his shoulders against the cold. He hung onto the side because the water was over his head. Holding his breath, and letting go of the side, he sank down under the water until he touched bottom. He came back up. The tinaja was about eight feet deep. Grabbing his flashlight, Morty got ready to retrieve the gold at the bottom of the tinaja. He didn't think there was enough room for him to easily dive down and he was afraid he might hit his head, so he decided it would be best to just dunk down to the bottom bending his knees and reach for the gold pieces. He shone the flashlight down into the water, but he'd stirred up some sediment and the water was murky, so he couldn't see where the gold lay or if indeed it was still there at all.

Perhaps the police had found it when they'd come back to make a thorough search of the area where Morty had been digging. The thought sent a chill down Morty's spine. Could all his effort be for naught? He dropped down to the bottom and reached down blindly with his hand. Groping around his hand brushed against something hard. He grabbed it and came to the surface. It didn't feel right. Lifting it up, Morty saw that it was a rock. He threw it away in frustration. Taking a deep breath, he decided to try to dive down headfirst after all.

Using his flashlight and putting his face right down near the bottom, he scanned the area illuminated by the beam while simultaneously groping through the accumulated debris with his left. He had to come up for air. Where was the gold? While he rested, Morty thought back to the night when he had dumped the gold in the tinaja. He tried to remember the exact spot where he'd overturned his backpack. He decided to try closer to the near edge. Diving down, he shone the light on the bottom near the wall – nothing. Moving the accumulated debris on the bottom, Morty caught sight of a sudden yellow gleam. He grabbed for it and coming to the surface, he saw it was indeed one of the gold coins. He set it on the rock and went down for more.

Excitement mixed with relief as he repeatedly dove down and came up with gold pieces. After half an hour of diving, Morty was exhausted. He stopped to rest – holding on to the edge of the tinaja. While he rested, he examined the gold pieces he'd brought up. It looked like he had gotten most of them, but he wanted to make sure. As valuable as the coins were, he sure didn't want to leave any behind. When he was rested, he dove down a few more times and came up with two more coins. He was pretty sure he had it all and in any case he was beat.

Morty scrambled out of the tinaja and took off his under trunks. He wrung them out and then put them back on. Despite the heat, he shivered for a spell. He wriggled into his jeans and put on his T-shirt. He emptied his pack and filled the large compartment with the gold pieces, then put the small flashlight in the front pocket with his food. When the water in the tinaja had settled, Morty filled up his water bottles and dropped a water purification tablet in each. He laid back and soaked up the rays of the sun. It felt glorious on his skin.

Morty took a different trail on his way back. As he walked along the base of a forty-foot tall cliff, he came to a valley oak tree that was literally growing out of and over a rock. Glancing upward through the branches, he spotted the mouth of a cave tucked high up on the cliff like a pillbox, hidden amid the upper branches of the giant oak. With the tree growing so close to the cliff, the cave was like a hidden treehouse, with a stone pillar at the fore. Morty climbed over and through the branches of the oak, using them to help him climb the twenty feet over the wind sculpted face of the massive sandstone cliff.

As Morty hoisted himself over the lip of the cave and into the dim space beyond, he heard a rattle. He froze. Silence. He looked around, slowly at first, then at ease when he realized there was no snake. Morty was sure he had heard a rattle though. He looked back at where he'd swung his feet up over the mouth of the cave. There was a locoweed growing there. Morty slid over and gave it a shake. The dry, woody seedpods gave a rattle that sounded remarkably like that of a rattlesnake. Morty examined the plant. He had read an article in *Ecology Magazine* about this very species. What was the scientific name? He searched his brain. He knew it was in there somewhere. *Astragalus asymmetricus.* That was it. Also known as the San Joaquin Milkvetch. Morty remembered that the article had stated that there are actually a number of different plants that are known as locoweed.

They got that name because they are poisonous when eaten by foraging animals in large quantities. Locoweed causes more poisonings of grazing herds of cattle, sheep, and goats than any other poisonous plant in the western United States. Depending upon how much locoweed was ingested and over how long a period of time, the animals may act crazy – hence the 'loco' in the name of the plants – exhibit signs of muscular weakness and paralysis, or die within a few hours. Some animals appear to recover from locoweed poisoning, however, they usually never quite have the same spirit. Morty wondered if any humans had ever suffered from locoweed poisoning. He wondered if he could get it to grow it in a pot. He gently twisted off a seedpod and put it in his pack. Morty thought it would make an interesting plant to study.

The cave stretched back, low-ceilinged. Morty crawled a few feet into the dark interior and sat down cross-legged He glanced around the five-foot high chamber as his eyes adjusted to the dim light. He closely scrutinized an object a few feet to his left. It was a mortar and pestle. In the base was a perfect bowl-shaped depression, and leaning against the side was the oblong, round-ended pestle. They must have been transported there from some other location for they were made of some black stone that was much harder than the sandstone. Morty could tell as much from the smoothness of their texture. Morty had brought along an oh zee of skywalker flowers – essential supply for the trip to his way of thinking. He took a couple of the purple buds out of a pouch and placed them in the mortar. Using the pestle, Morty ground the buds into particles fine enough to roll. He lit up.

The warm glow of Morty's lighter lit the walls of the cave and he caught a glimpse out of the corner of his left eye of a drawing on the rear wall. He held out his lighter to observe the artwork. Cross-like images with bright white bases edged in black appeared in the light of the lighter's flame. They had feather rays under the horizontal crosspieces and on their ends, like the underside of a bird in flight. The images were acephalic, left open to the heavens, four evenly spaced white plumes reaching out on top. Thick red columns, edged in black, stood on hills reaching up, open on top. Morty knew that the caves were sacred to Native Americans. He tried to imagine what the art symbolized to them. After having enjoyed a pleasant reverie for he knew not how long, Morty decided it was time to move on. He would have liked to stay longer in the amazing cave and cherish the view out over the golden hills, through the branches of the oak a while longer, but he was anxious to get safely back to his apartment with the gold.

Morty ascended a wind turbine festooned hill. The turbines stood like modern graven idols paying homage to the winds, stealing their power, spinning their energy into electricity. The whoosh whoosh whoosh of their tri-bladed rotors filled the air. They were touted as producers of energy that doesn't harm the environment. Except for the dead eagles and vultures. Never mind the concussed bat carcasses. Morty abhorred the abominable machines. As if the dead birds and bats were not enough, Morty felt the damned contraptions were an abomination on the landscape. The wind turbines were an eyesore encroaching upon the one place he cherished most in all the world. Morty had once hatched a plan to topple a dozen or so of the intruders that stood closest to some of his favorite caves, but in the end he decided it was best not to go tilting at wind turbines.

As Morty descended the foothills on his return trek, he came upon a stretch of level solid ground that was pocked with numerous water-filled depressions of various sizes and depths. As he wove a path along the high ground between them, it dawned on him what they were. He had read about vernal pools in a nature magazine not long ago. The rainy season had filled the pools with water and brought them back to life. Fairy shrimp cysts that had withstood heat and cold during the long period of desiccation had hatched out. They would grow to maturity in three to eight weeks. Eggs would be laid or preserved in the mother. The pool would begin to dry up again. A whole ecosystem from protozoa, rotifers, bacteria, and algae to tadpole shrimp, salamanders, frogs, and toads would develop in that brief period of time. The absence of fish as predators in these ephemeral ecosystems makes this a far more successful process than it would be in open waters. Over sixty species of plants, many of them endemic to specific pools, would grow, bloom, and germinate before the dry season ensued once more. One might see white meadowfoam, dwarf downingia, white-headed Navarretia, or colusa grass. Their insect pollinators would arrive, and the pools would be visited by delta green ground beetles, sandhill cranes, pocket gophers and multifarious hungry and thirsty animals.

Morty found vernal pools fascinating. He felt that it was a crying shame that many vernal pool environments in northern California had been destroyed by housing developments. Urban sprawl.

On his way out across the Byron Hot Springs property, Morty decided to give the spooky hotel building a wide berth. He'd seen more of the sad, eerie relic than he needed to on his way in and it had left an unpleasant impression upon him. In the moonlit darkness, he stumbled into a ring of rocks. In the murk, he could dimly perceive a water-filled depression beyond. Morty walked around the four-foot high ring of piled up rocks to an opening on the other side. He shone his flashlight on a large rock to the left. The words 'WHITE SULFUR' were chiseled into the base of it in capital letters. Steam was rising from the surface of the pool of water and the air was redolent of an acrid, musty odor.

Morty knelt down at the edge and put his hand in the water. It was quite hot – well over a hundred degrees, he judged. On an impulse, Morty set down his pack, took off his boots, and stripped off his clothes. He stepped down and waded in the spring. The pool was a ten-foot oval. The water came up to his thighs and it was so hot he could barely stand it. Nevertheless, he sat down quickly, immersing himself up to his shoulders. At first, it was hard to take, however Morty found that after awhile he could bear it if he sat perfectly still. He slid to the edge and leaned back against the rocks, his skin tingling with the movement. The intense heat rapidly relaxed his aching muscles and he began to feel like a limp garment draped upon the rocks. Morty still felt some tension in his neck and face, so he moved away from the edge and, holding his breath, he dunked down, completely submerging himself in the thermogenic spring. He could feel the heat easing the tension in his jaw and cheeks, at his temples, and along the back of his neck. He came up for air. He was used to the heat now and a euphoric sensation began to sweep over him. He sank under the water over and over. He laid back resting his head against a smooth, flat rock at the edge of the pool in a state of complete relaxation. He looked up at the stars, which shine especially brightly in the dark country.

Lying there in a state of bliss, Morty's thoughts drifted to the history of the place. It was strange to think that he was now soaking in the same hot spring that Lefty O'Doul, Clark Gable, Charlie Chaplin, and Jack London had soaked in three quarters of a century or so ago. He had read that the army had capped the curative waters of the spring during its tenure because the commander of the camp couldn't stand the 'rotten egg' smell of the sulphur. Somehow the water had found its way around the cap, as water will, and the spring flowed freely once again, filling the pool with its temperate water and the air with the odor of sulfur. Morty took a deep breath.

At one point while he lay soaking, Morty heard a couple of what he thought might be coyotes wrangling with each other not far away. Their close proximity was a bit unsettling, but he didn't imagine he was in any danger.

After having soaked in the hot spring for well over an hour and a half with brief periods of sitting at the edge in the cool night air, Morty decided it was time to get dressed and set up camp for the remainder of the night. As he emerged from the spring, he was a new man. All of his aches and pains from his exertions of the past few days had melted away and his body felt like a wet noodle cooked well past al dente. His skin was red all over. As Morty pulled on his clothes, he moved slowly, wishing to maintain the state of complete relaxation he was in.

Suddenly his heart leapt in his chest. Where was his backpack? He spun around scanning the ground; it wasn't there. Had he gone through all these trials only to lose the gold in the end? He racked his brain for an explanation, panic gripping his mind. He thought back. Yes, he had certainly put his backpack down right next to where he'd laid his clothes. It was gone. Could someone have crept up and stolen it while he was in the spring? It was hard to fathom. Morty examined the ground with his flashlight. He thought he could dimly perceive a trail of scraped away dirt as if the pack had been dragged along the ground. He followed it for about fifty yards, occasionally sweeping the ground ahead with the beam of the flashlight. Suddenly, the beam reflected off a green bundle. *My pack!*

Morty ran forward and sank to his knees before the pack. The outer pocket had been torn open. Morty hastily unzipped the large main compartment. *Whew!* He breathed a huge sigh of relief. The gold was still there. What had happened? His beef jerky. His beef jerky had been in the outer pocket and it was gone. *The coyotes!* The coyotes must have dragged his pack away and torn it apart to get at the beef jerky. *Thank heavens*, Morty thought. On the spot, Morty vowed to become a vegetarian – something he been considering for some time.

So much for maintaining his state of blissful relaxation. There was no way Morty would be able to sleep after what had happened, so he decided to hike on out to Byron Hot Springs Road and on into the town of Byron. It would be light before long and he could call for a taxi to take him back to Brentwood.

He came across the black sulfur spring. In the morning twilight, Morty contemplated the red lichen covered spring marker. 'BLACK SULFUR' was chiseled into the base like 'WHITE SULFUR' was on its marker. As Morty stared at the monolith, he thought he could see a face in the contours of its mass. Its countenance was a mirthful one. It reminded Morty of the Greek comedy mask. He knelt down and filled his water bottle from the tepid spring. He took a long drink before heading home.

When Morty got back to his apartment, he examined his treasure. He found three distinct types of gold pieces and separated them into piles. There were twenty-three of the same ten dollar horseman gold pieces dated 1850 like the three he'd first found. There were seven large octagonal ingots dated 1852. In the center of the obverse was stamped a defiant looking eagle perched on a rock – representing the constitution, Morty found out later – with its wings held high. A United States shield rested aslant the rock, the eagle holding arrows above the shield and an olive branch below in its talons. From the eagle's beak trailed a scroll with the word "Liberty" embossed upon it. Just above the eagle's head '887 THOUS' was stamped on a symmetrical scroll indicative of the degree of fineness of the gold. 'FIFTY DOLLS' was stamped below the rock at the bottom of the reeded circular central portion of the ingot, while the words 'UNITED STATES OF AMERICA' curved from left to right up and over the eagle. Along the eight sides at the outside of the ingot in a clockwise direction starting from the left were the words: 'UNITED, STATES, ASSAY, OFFICE, OF GOLD, SAN FRANCISCO, CALIFORNIA' and ending with '1852' at the bottom.

The reverse of the ingot was unlike any coin Morty had ever seen before. In the center was a series of twenty concentric circles of gradually increasing circumference like a target. These were surrounded on the outside by an embossed, web-like vignette extending almost to the eight sides. It had been engraved using a method known as engine turning.

Morty's subsequent research revealed that these fifty-dollar octagonal gold ingots, or quintuple eagles, were issued beginning in 1851 by the new federal assay office in San Francisco. The assay office functioned as a de facto mint, however its administrator, U.S. Assayer Augustus Humbert, did not have the facilities necessary to produce the ingots, so the work was contracted out to the most respected of the private coining firms, Moffat and Company. The heraldic eagle on the obverse was engraved by the well-known die engraver Charles Cushing Wright. The fifty-dollar ingots were only useful for large transactions, and the public was clamoring for smaller denominations, however, Humbert was not authorized by

Congress to produce them until early 1852. Once again, private firms stepped in to meet the public demand.

There were thirty-one gold eagles of the third variety. The obverse of these coins was virtually identical to the United States eagle design of Christian Gobrecht that appeared on the eagle for sixty-eight years from 1838 to 1907. It depicted a bust of Lady Liberty facing left with thirteen stars – representing the original thirteen states of the union – around the reeded perimeter and the date '1852' at the bottom. The only difference was that on the coins Morty had found the word 'LIBERTY' on her coronet had been replaced by 'MOFFAT & CO'. The eagle on the reverse was virtually the same as the one on the fifty-dollar ingots. On the scroll above the eagle '880 THOUS' was stamped. Around the reeded edge were: '264 GRS. CALIFORNIA GOLD' and at the bottom 'TEN D'. Morty later learned that 'GRS'. is an abbreviation of 'grains', that the grain as a unit of measurement was based on the weight of a grain of barley, and that two hundred and sixty-four grains is equivalent to slightly over six tenths of an ounce.

IV

Morty planned to take the gold pieces to Northwest Rare Coins and Bullion in Seattle. He trusted them to deal with him fairly as he felt certain they had in his previous transaction. He could also visit his father and pick up the rest of his things at his father's place. He made preparations for the road trip. Having so many valuable coins in his possession made Morty very anxious. He didn't dare leave them in his apartment unattended, nor did he dare to leave them in his car unattended. Fear of having the gold stolen was driving him mad. He had to get on the road soon. He planned to drive straight through.

Since he intended to be gone for at least two weeks, Morty decided to take Aura with him. Aura was the name he'd bestowed upon his beloved California mountain kingsnake. He made up a kind of traveling terrarium out of a sixteen-gallon clear plastic storage box. He cut an eight by twelve inch rectangular hole in the latching lid and duct taped a plastic screen over it for ventilation.

After Morty had packed his bags, he prepared the terrarium for its precious cargo. Once he had the soil mixture in place and a hollow wooden structure in which the snake could hide, Morty took Aura from her permanent home and put her into her travelling one for the first time. She would be fine. By the time he had loaded up the Jeep and gotten on the road, it was already late afternoon.

After having negotiated the traffic on five eighty west into Oakland, along the Eastshore Freeway through Berkeley and eighty east to Vacaville, across 505 to Interstate 5 north, and up to Redding, Morty was already exhausted. The adrenaline high generated by all the excitement of the past few days had completely worn off. He was beginning to nod off at the wheel. He had to stop. Morty exited five north and pulled into a restaurant parking lot. He reclined his seat and put his head back, almost immediately dozing off.

When Morty woke up, it was pitch dark. The only light came from the restaurant's sign. He was famished. He got out and pressed the smart key twice. The car emitted the expected beep. Morty walked into the Grizzly Bear Diner and sat down at the counter. He ordered coffee and, when it came, loaded it with sugar and a pour of cream. Morty drank three cups over the course of twenty minutes and had a slice of olallieberry pie. He was hungry, but he knew he would get groggy if he ate a big meal, and he wanted to press on. Glancing up, he saw red reflections flashing off the diner walls. He paid, walked out, and froze. A police cruiser and an ambulance were stopped behind his Jeep. The hatch of his Jeep was open. Morty ran over and looked in the back. The terrarium was right there where he'd put it. It was open.

"Excuse me, sir. Are you the owner of this vehicle?" the Redding police officer inquired.

"Yes, I am," Morty answered, looking at the officer and then glancing around behind him. A man on a stretcher was being loaded into the ambulance.

"It seems the man over there on the stretcher, a Detective Teufel of the Livermore Police Force, was searching your vehicle and got bitten by a venomous snake. He called nine one one raving about how he'd been bitten by a coral snake. He barely got out the words Grizzly Bear before he passed out. We found him on the pavement behind your vehicle. Is there any reason why you're transporting a dangerous reptile, son?"

Without answering, Morty started looking for the kingsnake. It wasn't in the terrarium. Morty briefly hefted the terrarium. He breathed a sigh of relief. The snake wasn't in the back of the car. He looked under the car and around the adjacent area on both sides and in front of the car. Where was Aura?

The cop was getting impatient for an answer.

"It's a kingsnake. They're completely harmless. Detective Teufel must be suffering from some kind of delusion, or shock, or something. I can assure you that there's no snake venom in his system."

"He'll be taken in for tests and administered an antidote if necessary. That is if an antidote to coral snake venom can be found."

"I told you, it's not a coral snake. It's a California mountain kingsnake. They look like coral snakes, but they're a native California species. It's a case of what biologists call Mertensian mimicry. The California mountain kingsnake's red, white, and black ring pattern is similar to that of a coral snake, but there are subtle differences in the pattern of the ring colors. What you have to remember is: 'Red and yellow, kill a fellow; red and black, venom lack'. That means that the snake is venomous if the red and yellow – or white – rings are touching in its pattern, but not if the red and black rings are touching. I'd show you if I could find my snake." He looked around some more. "These snakes actually eat rattlesnakes. They are immune to the venom of local venomous snakes."

The officer yawned and muttered, "Whatever." He continued, "You'll have to come down to the station to make a statement. We'll see how this plays out medically for Detective Teufel. Why would Detective Teufel want to search your car?"

"That's what I'd like to know. That can't be legal, can it?"

"We'll see. Follow me down to the station."

The ambulance departed for the hospital. Morty closed the liftgate of the Jeep and got in. He really wanted to spend more time searching for Aura. She might not have gotten too far. He hated to leave without her.

Morty gave his statement at the police station, then sat around waiting for two hours. Finally, the police sergeant, a Sergeant Givens, came over to inform Morty that Detective Teufel was recovering and that Morty had been right. Teufel had not been bitten by a coral snake, nor by any other poisonous snake. He had been bitten by a snake, but no venom was found in his system. "It's probable that believing he'd been bitten by a poisonous snake, he panicked and that may have triggered a mild heart attack. Apparently, Teufel has a heart condition." Teufel was recuperating but still in shock. He had not talked to the police as of yet, but Morty was free to go.

There was no way Morty could continue driving after the events of the past few hours. He had no choice but to get a motel room and get some sleep. He unloaded his bags, struggling to carry the heavy plastic terrarium into the room. There was one thing he did have to do before he crashed. Morty opened the terrarium and brushed aside a few inches of the substrate. The plastic wrapped gold pieces were still there all right. He stationed the terrarium between the bed and the wall, checked to make certain the door was locked, and fell on the bed like a crosscut sequoia.

The next morning after breakfast, Morty drove back over to the Grizzly Bear Diner to see if there was any chance of finding Aura. After searching the surrounding area in all the likely hiding spots for over an hour, he gave up. Morty reluctantly swung the Cherokee onto I-five north. A couple of hours later, as he was crossing into Oregon, Morty suddenly felt something slither over his left ankle. Aura! He pulled off at the next exit and picked her up. Aura loved to nestle in the warmth of Morty's lap. He decided to let her rest there for the remainder of their journey.

When Morty got to his father's home, they had a man-to-man talk. Morty apologized for lying to his father concerning the cross-country road trip. He tried to explain the intensity of his feelings, but found it difficult to account for many of his actions. One thing he did want to clearly convey, though, was that he was now a changed man. His priorities had been straightened out and he was in the midst of formulating a plan for his life. For the first time, Morty felt like he had the ambition to reach his goals whatever they might turn out to be. He showed his father the gold. Isaac Grunberg was dazzled speechless for the first time in his life.

V

Morty netted over five million dollars from auctioning off the rare gold coins. He immediately put away one million to pay his taxes. A few months later he went out to Byron to investigate a piece of property that was for sale. The owner had planned to develop the site as residential property. He'd made plans to level the property and build a dozen large upscale houses on large lots. Then his financial fortunes had taken a turn for the worse and he'd had to put the property up for sale.

As Morty walked the property with the realtor, he observed the familiar dry depressions on the tract. It was the very stretch of land he'd crossed on his return from his excursion to the Vasco Caves. If Morty didn't buy the land, it was likely that some other developer would and that the project would go forward. The depressions would be filled in and some of the last of the vanishing vernal pools would be lost forever. Morty's all-time favorite animal, the California tiger salamander, would return to breed and find its breeding ground replaced by lawns and mansions. They simply would not breed. As Morty stood looking over the desiccated pools, his inspiring visit to the Monterey Bay Aquarium came to mind.

Morty had a sudden subtle shift of consciousness – an epiphany, you might say. He would buy the land and found an institute for the protection of vernal pools. He would raise money and use it and the money he had to build a research lab and visitor center on a section of the property near Armstrong Road that was level ground and had no pools on it. Morty dreamed of being the first to successfully breed the California tiger salamander in captivity and increase its range by introducing it to more habitats. Morty bought the nineteen acre tract of land adjacent to the Vasco Caves Regional Preserve to the northeast, southwest of the old Byron Hot Springs Resort, and to the northwest of Byron Airport, for one point five million dollars.

Nine months later, the necessary permits had been procured and the plans had been drawn up. They broke ground on the institute building. It was to have a central reception area flanked by a gift shop on the right and a small natural history museum that could double as a classroom or conference room on the left. Behind the reception area was a central courtyard. A wing with five offices would extend back on the left side of the courtyard. A large laboratory would occupy the space along the back of the courtyard, with an outdoor research area where they could recreate the conditions of vernal pools out back. The right side of the courtyard was to be open with picnic tables where school groups and visitors could lunch and enjoy the view of the institute lands and Mount Diablo to the west. Raised redwood walkways would snake around the vernal pools on the property and serve as viewing platforms for guests.

The institute building would feature many state of the art green technologies. A living roof featuring native drought-resistant plants would cover the roof of the conference room, reception area, and gift shop, with an observation deck at the far end of the gift shop. Heliotropic photovoltaic solar panels would be installed on the roofs of the offices and laboratory. A rainwater catchment and filtration system was also in the plans for those two roofs. Skylights and expansive double-pane windows would provide natural illumination of the interior spaces during the daytime to reduce the use of electric lighting. A computer-controlled ventilation system would automatically open and close windows and skylights to regulate the temperature of the buildings and reduce dependence on heating and air conditioning systems. All of the walls were to be insulated with natural cotton batting made from recycled blue jeans. All of the materials used in the construction of the institute would be chosen for their sustainability and low environmental impact.

Morty wanted to demonstrate the values of the institute and its commitment to preserving the natural world by making the building design a shining example of energy efficiency and minimal environmental impact. Morty dubbed it 'the Vernal Institute'. He declared the institute a not-for-profit organization dedicated to the preservation of vernal pools and the endangered species that live in this ephemeral environment. Admission would be free.

Numerous critics of the Vernal Institute project argued that it wasn't worth the effort to build an institute solely devoted to the study and preservation of a biome that technically only existed during the wet months of the year, perhaps four of five months at best. Morty countered that that was the very reason the vernal pools were overlooked, undervalued, and in need of protection. He argued that the vernal pools are an integral part of the San Joaquin Valley ecosystem, and that they are an indicator of the health of the environment as a whole. Morty emphasized the need to take a global, four-season approach to conservation.

When asked what exhibits would be on display at the institute during the summer and fall when the vernal pools were desiccated, Morty replied that the Vernal Institute would create artificial vernal pool exhibits that could be studied year-round. In addition, the habits and living conditions of local frog, toad, and salamander species during the dry months would be observed and researched. Local flora and fauna of all species, native and invasive would be researched. The effects of introduced species of animals, such as the bullfrog, and plants, such as ryegrass would be studied. Native habitat restoration projects would be undertaken. Morty felt confident that the institute lands would prove to be fertile ground for scientific study, and that the public would appreciate the Vernal Institute's research, conservation, and educational efforts.

VI

January, 2000

The Vernal Institute opened shortly after the turn of the millennium with little fanfare, but it was an instant success. Somehow word had gotten out and a steady stream of visitors came. Many East Contra Costa County schools booked field trips. Numerous local people volunteered to be trained and serve as docents and research assistants. The institute received numerous generous donations. Even ol' Fritz Utrecht heard about Morty's success and donated ten thousand dollars. He had fully recovered from the rattlesnake bite. He had sold his Rolls Royce Phantom and was now driving a Prius. He'd lost weight and sold his coin shop. The new owner had renamed it Shasta Coins.

Morty enrolled at U.C. Davis and began taking classes with the objective of obtaining a B.S. in biology. Morty also learned a bit about fundraising and was able to procure several research grants. He'd hired two research biologists and they were developing research projects on fairy shrimp, tadpole shrimp, California red-legged frogs, western toads, and, of course, the California tiger salamander. Animal species that might be the subjects of future projects included the San Joaquin kit fox, the western burrowing owl, the loggerhead shrike, and the golden eagle. They were also planning a special study of the unique flora of these particular ephemeral pools. The Vernal Institute was off to a running start.

One summer day, Detective Ian Seare appeared at the institute. He asked to speak to Morty in private. In Morty's office, Seare congratulated Morty on the success of the Vernal Institute. Morty nodded and thanked him.

Seare said, "I wanted to let you know that I heard about the incident with Detective Teufel in Redding, and that on behalf of the Livermore Police Department, I would like to extend my deepest apologies for the criminal behavior of one of our officers. Detective Teufel has been kicked off the force, and is being prosecuted for graft. He is currently free on bail, awaiting his trial."

"Thank you for coming all the way out here to acknowledge and apologize for the wrongs committed by Teufel. I have great respect for you for taking the time to do that."

"It's the least I can do for you after all that's happened. It's so good to see that you've really made something of yourself."

"Thank you, Detective Seare."

"I wish you'd call me Ian from now on."

An uncomfortable silence followed, the two men staring at each other intently. Finally Morty said, "I really have to get something off my chest. I don't know what the consequences will be... I... I was responsible for my mother's death. It was an accident, I swear. I never intended to harm her. We were wrestling over the coins and when she tried to yank them away from me she fell and hit her head. I should have called nine one one..."

"Well, I suspected you early on. That day we hiked up to Brushy Peak pretty much sealed it. I knew you were lying. And there were other clues that pointed in your direction too, nothing that would stand up in court though, as we already found out."

"So what happens now?"

"Well, you've essentially confessed to a police officer and I should take you in, but I'm not going to do that. I believe you when you say that it was an accident, and yes you should have called nine one one, but in truth the blow to your mother's head was rather severe and I think she was killed instantly. In any case, I'm proud of you for what you've accomplished here and the direction in which your life is headed. I really don't want to do anything to disrupt that. I may be derelict in my duty, but I'm going to pretend we never had this conversation."

Extending his hand, Morty gave Ian a firm handshake and looking him straight in the eyes, he intoned, "Thank you, Ian."

Morty had advertised for a third research scientist to work at the institute. One of the applicants was a young Japanese American woman named Marisa Motoyama. Morty was surprised when she arrived for the interview riding a black and red Kawasaki motorcycle with her long black hair streaming out from under her red helmet, waving in the breeze. She dismounted and removed her helmet, then stood there in her tight-fitting black leather jacket, pants, and boots looking at him. Morty was smitten. She was stunningly beautiful. She stood proudly holding her head erect, her helmet under her right arm, her feet shoulder width apart and asked, "Are you Mr. Schwartzkopf?" When Morty replied in the affirmative, she introduced herself. "I'm Marisa Motoyama. I'm here for the research scientist interview."

"Yes, of course. Please come in," Morty somehow managed to breathe out. He led her to his simple yet tastefully furnished office. Morty found Ms. Motoyama to be a soft-spoken, demure woman, and it was plain from the interview and her résumé that she was an excellent research scientist. She had graduated magna cum laude from Cal with a B.S. in biology. She had grown up in the Central Valley and already had considerable experience studying vernal pool flora and fauna.

Morty's pet project was researching and breeding the endangered California tiger salamander. He had applied to the state of California for a license to breed California tiger salamanders and it had been granted. He was gratified when Ms. Motoyama demonstrated considerable knowledge of the species and showed great interest in his project. To top it off, Ms. Motoyama had considerable fundraising experience and was willing to assist with the fundraising duties of the institute on the condition that she could also participate in selected research projects. That would free up Morty to devote more time and energy to his California tiger salamander project while continuing to take care of the day-to-day running of the institute. All in all there was no question of whether or not Morty would hire Ms. Marisa Motoyama.

Marisa was particularly keen on the study of *Lasthenia conjugens*, the Contra Costa goldfields, and its symbiotic relationship with the solitary bees that pollinate it. She told Morty how these bees over winter underground, each in its own little sealed chamber where its mother laid its egg with a ball of goldfields' pollen, until the host plants flower in the spring. The bees instinctively know when the goldfields are in flower, and they emerge from their tunnel to fulfill their role as pollinators. During prolonged periods of drought when the goldfields don't flower, the bees wait patiently underground in a state of suspended animation for up to four years. Marisa was hoping to successfully restore *Lasthenia* to the institute lands where it had once thrived. It had been crowded out of most of its historic range by invasive species. *Lasthenia* gained federal status as an endangered species in 1997.

Marisa's facial features were not typically Japanese. Her pale skin tone and straighter, more prominent nose were due to her Okinawan descent, as Morty would later learn. Marisa parted her long, lustrous, black hair on the left with the greater portion sweeping down past her right eye. Often, she would reach up with her hand and flip her hair up over her head and let it fall back into place. On occasion, she would gather her hair in her hands at the back, flip it up and fix it behind her finely shaped head or twirl it about as she fixed it in a hairband to wear in a ponytail. These motions and looks captivated Morty. Almost as captivating was Marisa's knack for fundraising and her absolute competence as a research scientist.

After having worked closely together on fundraising, the salamander project, and the goldfields study for several months, Morty was completely and totally enamored with Marisa. They could work together comfortably for hours without speaking. When they looked in each other's eyes a spontaneous simultaneous smile broke out on each of their faces. There was a spiritual resonance between them. Finally there came a day when Morty could hold back no longer. He felt he would burst if he didn't ask Marisa out.

As he stood looking out over the Vernal Institute grounds from his office window, it began to rain. The wind and rain suddenly increased in intensity, blowing in in waves. The day he'd discovered the gold came to Morty's mind. He watched the water falling on the surfaces of the vernal pools scattered over the land. They were nearing their capacity now and were teeming with life. Marisa suddenly appeared by his side. She'd been thinking about their relationship for some time and she was sure Morty felt the same way she did. A woman knows these things. She knew Morty was too shy to ask so she took the bull by the horns. "Will you come to dinner at my place?"

A simple word. Only three phonemes. A short vowel sandwiched between two consonants. A single syllable.

Simple yet so hard to say sometimes. The implications of a commitment. I am willing to do what you ask. I will follow through. I will make it a reality. Morty finally found it easy to say. Yes.